P.C. HAWKE
mysteries

THE SQUARE ROOT OF MURDER

P.C. HAWKE
mysteries

THE SQUARE ROOT OF MURDER

PAUL ZINDEL

VOLO

Hyperion
New York

To Vincent, Ed—
and the dear, irrepressible Minnie

Copyright © 2002 by Paul Zindel

Volo and the Volo colophon are trademarks of Disney Enterprises, Inc.
All rights reserved. No part of this book may be reproduced or transmitted in any form or by any means, electronic or mechanical, including photocopying, recording, or by any information storage and retrieval system, without written permission from the publisher. For information address Volo Books,
114 Fifth Avenue, New York, New York 10011-5690.

Printed in the United States of America
First Edition
1 3 5 7 9 10 8 6 4 2

The text for this book is set in Janson Text 11.5/15.
Photo of thunderstorm: Don Farrall

Library of Congress Catalog Card Number on file.
ISBN 0-7868-1588-4
Visit www.volobooks.com

Contents

THE SQUARE ROOT OF MURDER • Case #5

Case #5 began something like this:

You can never be prepared for the truly unexpected—especially the unexpected disaster. In New York City, where I live, unexpected disasters seem to happen more often than most places: water mains burst, subway tracks catch on fire, taxis go out of control and crash into stores on Fifth Avenue. And of course, there are murders. Bodies of murder victims show up in the most bizarre places—in belfries, in refrigerators, faceup in herb gardens, facedown in kitty litter.

My pal and fellow detective, Mackenzie Riggs, and I have seen quite a few bodies in our day, especially since her mom is the New York City coroner, and we'd visited her at the morgue lots of times. But nothing could have prepared us for the unexpected and gruesome sight of our calculus professor impaled by an arrow against the blackboard of a Columbia University classroom.

How she came to be in that position is at the heart of one of our most challenging cases of all—one in which nothing seemed to add up . . . until we found ourselves staring into the face of pure evil.

Recording the truth and nothing but the truth, I am,

P. C. Hawke

(a.k.a. Peter Christopher Hawke)

A Class to Die For

It was a Saturday afternoon, the last fab and brill day of Indian summer. Mackenzie and I were sitting on a bench facing the Conservatory Water Pond, our favorite spot in Central Park. We watched the usual old salts operating their remote-controlled boats, trying to recapture their lost childhoods. Children ran around them, chasing each other and giggling. Mothers and nannies sat on benches, watching contentedly. But our minds were on something else—Henry Peachtree's recent suicide.

Henry had been a senior at Westside—a real achiever, with a golden future. But when he failed his science midterm and realized that he wasn't going to make it into Yale, he threw himself off his penthouse roof. Everyone said it was his mother who'd pushed him so hard to succeed. Pushed him right to the edge . . . and over.

"It's insane the kind of pressure parents put on their kids," Mac said. A lot of the people walking by were taking second looks at her because she was wearing a short black dress that had a violet snakeskin design sort of dripping all over it. The fact that she has long blond hair like Britney Spears's and a nose and eyebrows like Reese Witherspoon's didn't hurt either.

"No kidding," I answered. It's true. Every year, a few freshmen jump into the gorges at Cornell University in Ithaca because they can't take the strain. The same thing happens all over the world, especially in high-achieving, high-pressure places like Japan. But this was the first time something like this had hit so close to home. So it was no wonder we were in a freakazoid frame of mind that day.

In fact, even Mac and I weren't totally immune to academic pressures. We didn't feel pressure from our parents—believe me, teachers can be just as guilty. Take Mrs. Gilroy, our calculus teacher at Westside, for example. Back in September, she told all us juniors about an Advanced Placement Calculus class being given at Columbia University for gifted high-school students. You'd have thought Gilroy was our mother, the way she hounded me and Mac to take the class.

I guess we were doing considerably better than most of our classmates, but, jeez! At any rate, Mac and I decided it couldn't hurt to develop our problem-solving and logic skills for our detective work. So that's how we ended up at the ivy-covered campus of Columbia every Wednesday afternoon that fall, from four to six P.M.

Mackenzie and I were no slouches at Westside, which

is a pretty demanding school. But we weren't quite prepared for the variety of freaks, kooks, and eccentric geniuses who'd signed up for our new class. And believe me, we'd already met our fair share of weirdos at our school.

In fact, some of them had signed up along with us. Myrna Zareski, for example. She'd gotten a 1590 on her SATs in ninth grade, then swallowed a whole bottle of aspirin because she'd missed one question. She was better now, but that was only after a whole lot of expensive therapy.

Then there was Martin Hong Lee. When Westside's board was going to hire a consultant and pay him $100,000 to set up a whole new computer network, Martin had walked into the office and told the principal he'd already done it, in his spare time, for fun, and gave it to the school free of charge. For Myrna and Marty, this class was pretty much a piece of cake—just another notch on their belts on the way to M.I.T., Stanford, Harvard, or Yale.

But neither Myrna nor Marty was even among the top-ten wackiest ducks in our class at Columbia. There was some pretty stiff competition for that dubious honor, believe me.

"Speaking of students under strain," I said, "how about Bernadette Lello? It's a shame, the way that poor kid's being exploited." Bernadette, or "Bernie," as everyone called her, was only eleven years old. She was definitely the Columbia group's resident genius—although Professor Dunaway seemed to have her doubts. Her dad, who was also her manager and agent, had gotten Bernie on a few TV and radio talk shows. Heck, he'd even had a creepy "Girl Genius Web Site" featuring her as a pint-sized environmental crusader created for her, and promoted it every chance he got.

"Really," Mac said. "She needs to get a life, and her dad needs to take a chill pill. Do you think she has any friends at all?"

"Beats me," I said, shrugging. "I don't see how she could have."

"I'll tell you, though—for sheer stress and strain, I think Gabby Zoole takes the cake."

I had to admit that Gabby was a truly strange brain, even among the cuckalooney birds who had flocked to the class. She had hair like wet linguini, and a personality to match. According to Mac, Gabby looked as if she went out of her way to pick styles of dresses made from chicken-feed bags. I thought they went well with her weird, thin lips.

"Myrna says her hobby is medieval weaponry."

"No kidding?"

"Apparently she's got quite a collection of curiosities at home."

"I can believe it," I said. "I mean, have you checked out those NRA buttons she wears to class?"

"'Guns don't kill people, people kill people?'"

"Cheery thought, right?"

"It might help if she smiled once in a while," Mackenzie said, shaking her head.

There were plenty of other pubescent oddities in the class, but I'll get around to them later. First, I've got to tell you what happened that day in the park, because looking back on it, it was our first indication that something bad was about to happen.

So we were sitting there gossiping about our dorky classmates and the pressure we were all under when we spotted our calculus professor for the Columbia course, Professor Dunaway, on the other side of the pond.

If there was ever a teacher who put pressure on her students, it was Eva Marie Dunaway. She never missed an opportunity to make a cruel comment about a student. All of us had felt her sting—even little Bernie Lello. For some reason, it really seemed to stick in Dunaway's craw that Bernie was so smart. Maybe it bothered her that Bernie figured out the answers to nearly all the problems she set without writing anything down. Dunaway tortured the poor kid with constant snide comments. But then, that was her style with everybody. A couple of times even I wanted to get up and strangle her in front of the whole class. I don't think there was a kid in the room who didn't feel that way at one time or another. And now, here she was, walking in our direction.

"Hey," Mac said, nudging me. "Do you see what I see?"

"It's Pythagoras in a wig, all right," I replied. "And who's that guy she's with?"

"I don't know. But they look awfully cozy, don't they?"

"They sure do," I agreed, watching the couple strolling around the pond, arm in arm. "Do you think it's her husband?"

"I didn't think she was married," Mac said, perking up. "Interesting . . ."

The couple came closer, and as they did, Professor Dunaway withdrew her arm from the man's, and the pair began to argue. It was a pretty heated argument, too, judging from their body language.

"Do you think we should say hi?" I asked.

"No way," Mac said. "This looks pretty nasty. I think we should get a little closer and see if we can hear what they're saying."

"You're on," I said. We got up, and meandered slowly toward them, keeping our faces averted so Dunaway wouldn't recognize us. Although, come to think of it, I was pretty sure she wouldn't recognize us outside the familiar confines of her classroom. Professor Dunaway was like that, totally fixated on whatever she was doing at the moment. And right now, she was busy arguing with the man by her side. We could have walked right up to them, and she probably wouldn't even have noticed.

As we passed the couple, we got a good look at the guy Dunaway was with. He was balding, but not bad-looking—tall and slim, with regular features. At the moment he was trying out an ingratiating smile on the professor. We did a quick one-eighty and trailed them at a distance of about fifteen feet.

"Come on, Evie, don't take it that way," he said.

"How should I take it?" Dunaway said, pulling her arm away as he tried to grab it again. "You led me on."

"That's just not true, and you know it," the man said. He put his hand on his chest to show how hurt he was by her accusation. "How can you forget all the times we—"

Dunaway brushed this aside with a contemptuous flick of her hand. "You told me you were going to leave your wife."

"Well, as it happens, she's leaving soon—next week, in fact. Leaving the country."

"Oh, really? When did this happen?" Dunaway stopped walking, as if taken by surprise, and of course, so did we. Then she said, "I just can't trust you anymore, Harry."

"Please, Eva Marie . . . don't be like that. . . ."

Mac and I couldn't catch every word, but we're well trained to snoop. We'd honed our eavesdropping skills hanging around crime scenes, where it can be excruciatingly important. Under stress, people often say all kinds

9

of things that turn out to be useful later. Anyway, to make a long story short, Dunaway switched gears and started grilling this Harry guy about some investment his company was making for Columbia.

Then it looked like Harry was blowing more smoke up Dunaway's skirt, telling her that his company was making the university great dividends—stuff like that. You know, a regular salesman's pitch, but we could tell it wasn't fooling Dunaway one little iota. Her icy voice cut through his excuses just as it did in class when some poor kid couldn't answer one of her questions.

"Blah, blah, blah! That's three million of our money you've got there, Harry. As a consultant to the committee, I'm going to demand a more detailed accounting."

"Yes, yes, in a few weeks you'll see a detailed quarterly statement—"

"I'd better."

"You will. But, Evie, let's not let this get in the way of our relationship—"

"And it had better be *fully* detailed, or you and Americom will be sorry."

"It will be, I promise. But Evie—"

"Don't 'Evie' me! I'm not having it anymore, Harry. Our 'relationship,' as you call it, will be strictly business from now on. And I'm warning you, I'm going to be watching Americom like a hawk."

Dunaway did a quick about-face and marched right past Mackenzie and me, with one last parting shot over her shoulder. "And keep that psycho daughter of yours away from me!"

Mackenzie grabbed me by the arm. "I think it's time we went home, don't you?"

I did. And *we* did. The last thing I saw as we quick-stepped away was Harry, Professor Dunaway's mystery romance, frozen on the path. His face looked a lot like the way kids in our class looked when Dunaway singled one out for extra abuse—a combination of fear . . . and murderous rage.

2

Tea Without Sympathy

On the Sunday afternoon after our third class, we were all invited to a tea in the math department's faculty lounge, so that our parents could meet Professor Dunaway. I was feeling pretty cool in a pair of new dark-blue chinos and a crew-neck sweater that made me look as if I really work out. I'd gelled my hair so it looked straighter than usual—some new stuff that tornado winds wouldn't budge.

Mackenzie and I took a cab uptown to Columbia with her mom. Mrs. Riggs is a New York City coroner, and her professional connections and expertise have come in handy on several of our cases. Mac's dad, Dr. Riggs, couldn't make it that day. He's a famous psychiatrist, and he sees his clients on Sunday afternoons.

My dad couldn't make it either. He's the head archaeologist at the American Museum of Natural History, and that week, he was off in the Gobi Desert on an assignment. He's always traveled a lot for his job, but he's been doing it more than ever since my mom died about two years ago. I took her death pretty hard, but it left Dad in much worse shape. He hasn't been the same since. Although lately, I have to say, he's seemed a little more lively. I was glad that he was coming out of his gloom.

"My goodness," Mrs. Riggs said as we strode up College Walk, past ivy-covered walls, onto the enclosed main quadrangle of the university. "It's so peaceful here—like an island in the middle of the city."

For a second I was afraid she'd been about to say "like my morgue." There was no place she'd rather be. Mac and I had gotten used to visiting her there, but it was hard not to be a little creeped out by the place. "I'm surprised you've never been here before," I said.

"Yes, you'd think I'd have gotten up here by now, considering my line of work," she agreed. "But Columbia's pretty crime free."

Talk about famous last words.

The three of us made our way to the math department lounge in the Euclid Building, just to the right of the library, where the faculty tea was already in full swing. The room was crammed with people—maybe fifty in all—but the first person to catch our attention was Professor Dunaway.

Tall, with short-cropped blond hair and piercing blue eyes, Dunaway was, as always, an imposing presence. No one ever stood up to her without being cut down to size. Just the week before, Mac and I had heard her screaming her head off at Jeremiah Jones, one of our classmates. At the moment he was standing by the buffet, wolfing down canapés. I don't know how he managed to do that without swallowing his tongue ring.

Next to Jeremiah was Natalie Baker, his girlfriend. As usual, they were wearing matching leather jackets to go with their matching rings—except hers were in her eyebrow and her navel. She liked showing off her belly ring by wearing those tight low-rider jeans. Mac sniffed disapprovingly to me in an aside. "Check out the Bobbsey twins."

I grunted. "Egads!"

Jeremiah and Natalie had big plans, and made no secret of them. They were going to march off to Harvard together next year, to higher academic and romantic bliss. But apparently, things weren't going as planned. On our way to class last week, Mac and I had overheard Dunaway and Jeremiah going at it.

"My recommendations, or lack thereof, can make or break your academic future, young man," Dunaway had shouted. "Harvard won't have you if I give the thumbs-down."

"Look, lady," Jeremiah had yelled, "Natalie's already been accepted. I'm going to Harvard with her, and nobody—not you or anyone else—is going to stop me!"

"We shall see about that. Meanwhile, take my advice: stop thinking Harvard, and start thinking Hofstra!"

There was a strangled, furious sound, then a booming thud as something hard hit the concrete floor.

"Throwing textbooks will get you nowhere, Jeremy

"It's Jeremiah, I told you." His voice was soft yet sim-mering, probably trying to sound like a junior Al Pacino. "And you'll be sorry if you cross me."

From the looks on their faces now as they laser-beamed Dunaway with their eyes, Jeremiah and Natalie were still steaming at Professor Dunaway.

Mrs. Riggs, Mackenzie, and I gave the two of them a wide berth and mingled for a while. I waved at Myrna and Marty, our classmates from Westside, who were sip-ping punch over by the windows. Gabby Zoole was with them. Most of the kids in the class avoided Gabby like the bubonic plague, but Myrna and Marty are pretty open-minded and accepting. At a school like Westside, you had to be.

After about half an hour, Mrs. Riggs got a page, and told us she had to get to a crime scene ASAP. "They've got a corpse down in Chinatown," she explained, hand-ing Mac some cab fare and money for dinner. "Sorry to rush away like this, but you know how it is."

"S'okay, Mom," Mackenzie said, giving her a kiss on the cheek.

"Your professor's a very . . . interesting lady," Mrs. Riggs said, raising her eyebrows meaningfully.

"Mmm." Mac made a wry face. "We'll talk. 'Bye, Mom."

The tea was going along pretty smoothly, considering all the yelling we'd become used to during the first three weeks of class. Professor Dunaway continued holding court, in her irritating, superior way, schmoozing with all the parents. And they were lapping it up, too. All except a red-faced man standing in the back of the group of parents. He looked like he'd just eaten a red-hot pepper and was about to explode.

I nudged Mackenzie. "Who's that?"

She shrugged. "Let's go check it out."

We edged closer, sensing a drama in the making. The red-faced man pushed his way to the front of the crowd. "Could I have a word with you about your grading system, Professor?" he rumbled.

Dunaway looked him up and down. "I hardly think this is the time, Mr. Lello."

"*I need to speak with you!*" His enraged bellow shattered the polite, social murmuring that filled the room. All around the lounge, heads turned. Over in the corner, I saw Bernadette hunch down in her chair. She was sitting by herself, as usual. I felt sorry for her. How could she possibly have any normal social skills, the way her father paraded her around? I wondered how her mother felt about the whole thing.

"Very well," Dunaway replied. "But as you can see, I'm very—"

"Yes, I'm sure you're busy," he said, "but not too busy to be *sued*!"

"I beg your pardon?" she said, seeming genuinely surprised.

"Yes," he said, nodding. "For slander and incompetence!"

"Mr. Lello!"

"Don't 'Mr. Lello' me," he said, trying in vain to keep his voice down. "Bernadette has never, *ever*, gotten any grade below an A in her entire life. Her mother and I—not to mention our attorney—think this is very fishy, especially considering the resistance you put up to having her in your class at all."

"Yes, well, perhaps I should explain."

"Yes. Perhaps you should." Mr. Lello folded his arms in front of him, his eyes locked on her like twin daggers.

"It's true that your daughter has a photographic memory," Dunaway said. "But beyond that, her gifts are rather ordinary."

Lello started blustering, but she silenced him by raising a hand. "As I was saying, Bernadette is simply a bright girl in my opinion—not by any means a genius, as you have made her out to be. In fact, her intellect seems to me to be altogether mediocre."

"Now, look here—" Lello said. But she cut him off again.

"I know you have been packaging her as an intellectual circus act," Dunaway continued. "Television and radio appearances and such. But believe me, she has great limits. And she is using her memory to compensate. That can take her only so far and no farther. She really has no place on this campus, Mr. Lello. She should remain in sixth grade at the Dalton School, where she belongs."

"Just what have you got against her?" Lello barked, his hands gripping into white-knuckled fists at his sides.

"I don't believe in pushing children beyond their capabilities, Mr. Lello. If the Dean hadn't personally ordered me to take her, Bernadette would not have set foot in my classroom." Dunaway snorted. "Apparently, he felt the university could benefit from the publicity of having her here. But please—do not complain about her grades. C's are generous, believe me. I personally think she may well fail my course, and I intend to veto her scholarship to the university for the fall semester."

For a brief moment, Lello looked like he was going to punch her. Then he spun on his heels, grabbed poor Bernie by the wrist, and dragged her out of the room.

Holy kamozes. It seemed like a lot of people were angry with Professor Dunaway.

"Poor kid. Can you imagine what it must be like having parents like that?" I whispered to Mac.

"Yeah. Did you see the look on her face? She looked like she wanted to sink right through the floor."

Dunaway, on the other hand, looked as if she had actually enjoyed the scene. She stood there with an amused, supercilious look on her face. Everyone else just stood around as if they were shell-shocked. Luckily, the uncomfortable silence was interrupted by the sound of the lounge door flying open. We all turned to see who the late arrival was.

"Sorry I couldn't make it earlier," the man said breathlessly, flashing a sheepish grin. "Hello, everybody, I'm Harry Zoole—Gabby's father."

"Omigod, it's him," Mac whispered in my ear. "It's the guy who was with Dunaway in the park!"

"Gabby's father," I said, sucking in a big breath of air. "Gee, Mac, how's your scalp feeling now?" Whenever the skin on top of Mackenzie's head tingles, it can only mean one thing—something's definitely wrong. We've come to rely upon this strange manifestation, because it's never failed to be accurate.

"About eight-point-three on the Richter scale," she said. "The kind of usual tingle before we find a dead body."

It was a joke, of course, and we both chuckled at Mackenzie's black humor. If we'd only known then what was about to happen, we wouldn't have found it funny at all.

Sneak Attack

The next Wednesday was our fourth class, and Professor Dunaway was late—a first, since usually she was there way before anyone else. Jeremiah and Natalie were taking advantage of the moment to diss Bernadette Lello.

Bernie was sitting at a desk, staring at one of the class's desktop computers. She was wearing a pair of glasses with oversized frames and lightly tinted pink lenses. Jeremiah and Natalie obviously thought they were a hoot—which, to be honest, they were. Still, that was no excuse for the way the obnoxious twins were acting.

"C'mon, lemme try 'em on!" Jeremiah begged, trying to pull them off Bernie.

"No-o-o! They're mine, and they're very expensive!" she complained, pushing his hands away.

"I *have* to try them on!" he pleaded. "They're so super-stylish! Neat-o keen! Cool!"

Natalie snorted with laughter. How attractive. Not.

I could see Bernie's shoulders heave, and her chin started to quiver. I'd had about enough. "Knock it off!" I told Jeremiah and Natalie.

"Aw, P.C. gotta crush on little Bernadette?" Jeremiah mocked.

"Shut up, loser," Mackenzie jumped in. "Why don't you go pick on someone more your mental speed? Like at the gorilla cage at the zoo!"

Jeremiah and Natalie exchanged an eye roll, but they did back off, still screeching with laughter.

"You okay?" I asked Bernie, as Mac gently patted her shoulder.

"I—I guess so," Bernie said. Her voice was shaky and she blinked rapidly, still staring at the computer. The screen showed a jazzy graphic announcing

BERNIE'S HOME PAGE
WELCOME, CYBER-TRAVELER!
YOU HAVE REACHED THE
ECOLOGICAL GIRL GENIUS WEB PAGE.

As I said before, the Web site was a little creepy. Bernadette came off as this eerily perfect, plastic, packaged person, almost like that robot in *A.I.* It was kind of sad how much her parents must have capitalized on her brains and created this icky, shiny-happy image. Talk about pressure!

"High tech," Mac commented. I knew Mac was thinking what I was thinking, but she always came out with the right thing to say. I could tell she had a soft, mothering spot for Bernie.

"Thanks," said Bernadette. "My dad had the best Web-design company in New York create it."

"It must be scary to be so famous at such a young age," I said, trying to draw her out a little.

Bernie looked uncomfortable. "A little, I guess. But my dad says you can never start a career too early."

I didn't want to say anything negative about her so-called "career," so I changed the subject. "Are those special lenses or something? They look kind of . . . different."

"They're especially for working on the computer," Bernie explained. "They cut down on glare from the screen. I just got them."

"Wow," I said. "I didn't know they made glasses for that. I thought they just made those antiglare screens. Can I take a look?"

"I don't know . . . they might get stretched. . . ."

"Oh. Well, okay. They're pretty cool, though," I assured her.

"Really?"

"Definitely," Mackenzie said. "Jeremiah and Natalie were just being jerks."

"Well, I guess you two guys should know about what's cool and what's not," Bernie said, beaming at us. "I heard you're real practicing detectives! Is it true?"

"Um, I guess you could say that," I said.

"We've solved a few surreal cases," Mac admitted.

"Myrna and Martin told me you solved a murder case at the Museum of Natural History? They said it was even in the newspapers."

"True," Mac said.

"Guilty as charged," I added.

"That is so awesome!" Bernie said. "I'd love to be a detective, too! Do you think I could help you guys on a case sometime?"

"Uh, sure, I guess," I said, just to calm her down. "Sometime . . ." The thought of Bernie Lello working on a case with us didn't exactly thrill me. From the look Mackenzie gave me, I could tell she wasn't wild about the idea either. Luckily, we were saved from any bizotic commitments when Professor Dunaway finally showed up.

"Sorry I'm late," she said. "It won't happen again, I promise you." She cast a cold glance around the room. "All right, class, let's get to work. And I hope you'll pay better attention than you did last week. Please pass these sheets around. You've heard of pop quizzes? Well, this is a pop *test*."

The test was a major one, four pages long, and I blanked on just about every other question. Looking around, I saw that Mackenzie had a dazed expression on her face, as did most of our classmates. Only Myrna, Martin, and Bernadette Lello were scribbling away as if it were just a day at the beach.

After class, Bernie followed me and Mac as we headed for Broadway and the downtown subway. "Hey," she asked us, "how'd you guys do on the exam?"

"Not too great," Mac said.

"Nightmarish," I chimed in.

"Well, I could give you a little tutoring, if you want," Bernie offered. "Since we're like, friends now, and since you're going to let me help you with your next case?"

"Um . . . well, that's nice of you, Bernie," I began, trying to find a nice way to avoid a commitment. Bernie was okay, but I for one didn't want her as a detective partner. That would be like recruiting a Chihuahua for a guard dog.

Mackenzie, though, seemed to think the bargain was worth it. "We could use the help," she said, looking at me with pleading eyes, as if to say, "It's always better to be kind."

I wasn't so sure. Being kind now might mean letting Bernie down harder later, when we told her we didn't want her kibitzing on our criminal cases. But I wasn't about to stand up to the both of them together. Not then. And not there, at the top of the subway steps, with the cold north wind sweeping down Broadway and inside my coat, making me shiver. "Okay, I guess."

"Terrific!" Bernie said brightly, clapping her gloved hands together. "How about we meet in the computer lab next Wednesday, maybe half an hour before class?"

"*Très* cool," Mackenzie said, clapping Bernie on the arm. "See you then, huh?"

"Yes!" she said, and ran off, trailing her book bag and pigtails behind her.

"Cute kid, huh?" I said, watching her go. "Perfect

helper for a homicide case."

"I feel sorry for her, don't you?" Mac asked me.

"Yeah. With all her brains, fame, and money, I still wouldn't trade places with her for anything." I slapped myself across the face. "What am I saying? I'm probably going to end up discovering the wonders of deep frying, secret sauces, and minimum wages."

As it turned out, our first tutorial session with Bernie was enlightening, to say the least. Too bad we hadn't gotten together with her a week earlier.

Dunaway started off that day's class by reading our test scores out loud. "These are some pretty pathetic results from some supposedly strong brains. I'm more than disappointed. I'm disgusted." The marks ranged from a high of 78 percent (Myrna and Bernie) to a low of 46 percent (Jeremiah). Most of us were in the sixties—half above that magic 65 percent, and half below, including me and Mac.

Finding out our scores that way was humiliating enough, but Dunaway seemed to take special pleasure in rubbing it in. "I know what you're all thinking, that it was a surprise test, with no chance to go home and memorize mountains of information. But that is just the point, class: calculus is not about memorizing numbers."

Here she looked directly at Bernadette, who turned bright red. "It is about learning to think and to reason!"

Mac and I looked at each other, and simultaneously shook our heads. Several people started muttering under their breath.

Professor Dunaway continued her attack. "There is no room for weak cretins in higher mathematics. Only the strong intellects survive, so don't go looking for me to grade you on a curve. If the best student in this class rates a C, that student will get a C, and the rest of you will get what you deserve."

The lamentations of the class grew louder. "You'll get what *you* deserve, too," Jeremiah muttered.

"We're not doing moronic math any longer, class. The main reason most of you did so poorly was awesome laziness. I am furious that no one paid attention to my strict instructions, always, to round all calculations off to the nearest hundred thousandth." Dunaway stalked to the front of the room and drew .00000 in huge zeroes across the board. The squeak of the chalk made us all wince.

"And now let's get on to today's lesson." After a moment of stunned silence, we settled down to take notes. The subject of the day was differentiation, which I won't even try to explain, because I'm not too sure I get it myself, or ever will.

"If an arrow is fired from a distance," Dunaway said, "we could constantly halve the partial distance the arrow travels in a fraction of a second, and then halve the next partial distance, and the next and the next, infinitely—so that, in theory, the arrow would never reach its target. Isn't that right, Gabby?"

"I . . . I guess so," Gabby Zoole stammered, taken aback. "I'm . . . I'm not sure."

"Why, Gabby, I thought you knew all about arrows," Professor Dunaway said, cocking her head sideways. "Aren't you some kind of medieval-weapons expert?"

"I—yeah, sort of, I guess." Gabby squirmed as Dunaway approached her, and hovered over her desk.

"Why, I picked that example just for you, dear. I thought, If she understands nothing else in this class, at least she'll understand about arrows." Dunaway turned on her heels and strode slowly back up the aisle. Behind her, Gabby Zoole gave her a look that made it obvious just where she'd like to shoot that arrow. It made me wonder if she knew about Dunaway's frolics with her father, or if she just hated getting picked on.

"Jeremiah," Dunaway said, stopping beside him. The pierced wonder, who'd been quietly laughing at Gabby's discomfort, froze in his seat. "Perhaps you can elaborate on differentiation for us."

"I . . ."

"Perhaps not, then," Dunaway continued. "Well, I'd be happy to write you a recommendation for a community college. Perhaps you could take a remedial class there next year."

For once, Jeremiah had no answer. He looked down and dug his pencil into his notes, violently crossing things out, pressing so hard that the pencil snapped in two. Natalie put her hand on his arm, but he yanked it away.

Dunaway ignored this bit of byplay and continued her lecture on differentiation. By the time the class mercifully ended at 6 P.M., she had singled out most of the kids for personal humiliation, me and Mackenzie included. As we gathered up our books to go, Professor Dunaway fired one last parting shot. "I hope you'll all be better prepared for the next class."

The next Wednesday, Mackenzie and I met Bernie for our second preclass get-together in the computer room. I was really looking forward to it. The week before, Bernie had helped me raise my homework grade from a C to a B. The midterm test was looming, so I desperately wanted to pick her brains.

Bernie was waiting for us. When we got to the computer room at 3 P.M., she was sitting in front of her laptop, staring at the screen through her special glare-deflecting glasses.

"Hi, guys!" she greeted us cheerfully. "How was your week?"

"Fabulously dull," Mac said, sitting down on Bernie's left as I took the chair on her right.

"Any new detective cases?" Bernie asked hopefully.

"Not yet," I said, trying hard not to grimace at the prospect of teaming up with an eleven-year-old brainiac.

"We sure could use some help on a few of those equations Professor Dunaway gave us, though," Mac said, steering the conversation back to safer ground.

The three of us went over several of the problems until exactly 3:46. I remember the time because I looked up at the clock after we heard what sounded like a gunshot. Then there was a sharp *thwack!* from our classroom down the hall. Seconds later, somebody screamed: "Oh, my God. Help! I think she's dead!"

Safety in Numbers—Not

She turned out to be Professor Dunaway. And she was dead, all right. No doubt about it. The first thing Mac, Bernie, and I saw when we got to the classroom door was Eva Marie Dunaway standing with her back pinned against the blackboard. A short, steel-shafted arrow was protruding from her chest. Eyes wide open in horror, she looked surprised, as if she couldn't believe the speed with which she'd been impaled.

Whatever the theory of differentiation says about the flight of an arrow, in reality, they always reach their targets. It was, let me tell you, a totally grisly sight.

Mackenzie and I, having been through quite a bit of mayhem in our lives, are a little more together than most people when the unexpected disaster hits. It took us a few seconds of frozen staring, but we were certainly a lot more braced than anyone else on the scene.

Several members of the faculty were attempting to remove Professor Dunaway from the blackboard, but they weren't having much luck. "Leave her alone," I told the teachers. "This is a crime scene. You shouldn't touch anything!"

Mackenzie pointed to the crowd of people about to barge into the classroom. "You've got to keep everybody out! And get the police!" That seemed to wake up the trio of professors, who suddenly transformed themselves into efficient, authoritarian traffic cops. They seemed relieved not to have to look at the body anymore.

Having secured the room for the moment, I turned my gaze to follow the trajectory the arrow must have taken. Mackenzie and I reached the window at the same moment, and found ourselves staring at a big, old evergreen tree that stood just outside the window. Its main trunk was only ten feet or so away, and strong, sturdy limbs branched off in all directions. A perfect tree to climb. A perfect vantage point for the murderer.

There was no one in the tree. Whoever had shot Dunaway was long gone. Looking down, I saw something glinting on the ground in the afternoon sunshine. Even from this distance, I could tell that it was a crossbow.

"Do you see what I see?" I whispered to Mackenzie.

"We'd better get down there before somebody else grabs it," she muttered back.

When we turned to go, I caught sight of Bernadette. She was standing at the back of the classroom, staring in horror at Professor Dunaway's corpse. She seemed totally freaked out, in a state of shock. Her eyes were blinking rapidly, and her hands were twitching as they rested on top of one of the classroom's desktop computers. She looked like she would fall to the ground if the computer wasn't there to hold her up.

I signaled to Mac. "Let's bring her with us."

"Absolutely," Mac agreed. She took Bernie's hand and pulled her through the crowd still gathered at the door. We hustled her down the stairs, and out into the chilly late November air. The sun was just setting, casting deep shadows on the quad and the trees that lined the campus buildings.

The crossbow was still there, lying between the trunk of the tree and the building. I crouched down beside it, but was careful not to get too close. I didn't want to contaminate or disturb any markings, footprints, or other clues.

"Have you got your flashlight with you?" I asked Mackenzie, who was standing on the brick path with her arm around Bernie's shaking shoulders.

"Always," Mac said, flashing me a grin and taking her minilight out of her leopard-spotted backpack. She tossed it to me, and I played it on the ground around the tree. Sure enough, there were muddy footprints. Mine, of course, but someone else's, too. Someone wearing what looked like hiking boots. One set of prints led up to the tree, and another set back away from it.

It was obvious what had happened: someone had

climbed up with the crossbow, shot Professor Dunaway through the open window, then climbed or jumped down. They'd left the crossbow, either in their hurry or on purpose, and fled the scene.

The crossbow itself was not like the molded plastic and steel ones you see in outdoorsman stores. This one was made out of carved wood. It looked like an imitation antique crossbow. Maybe even the real thing, I thought, remembering Gabby Zoole's fascination with medieval weaponry.

Perhaps the murderer hadn't fled the scene after all. Maybe he, or *she*, was still around. The sound of sirens close by pierced my thoughts. "Good," I said. "Finally. Mac, you stay here with Bernie and make sure no one disturbs the site. I'll go back upstairs and see what I can find out from the police."

"Hey!" Mackenzie protested. "How about *I* go up, and *you* stay here?

"Okay," I said. "Let's both go. Bernie, you can keep an eye on the crossbow."

Bernie looked terrified. "You mean nobody's going to stay with me?"

Mac was the first to cave. "Oh, okay, P.C. You go."

"Right," I told her, giving her a wink that I'm sure she didn't appreciate.

I headed back up to the crime scene, and got there just as the police were taping off the room. There were still a lot of people milling around: professors, students, and curious onlookers. Maybe even the murderer, I thought, eyeing Gabby.

I couldn't talk my way back inside, but at least that meant that the murderer couldn't, either. Whatever evidence was inside the classroom was safe now. Mac and I had reached the classroom too fast for the murderer to have gotten there ahead of us, and we'd cleared the room quickly. The police would find the crime scene pretty pristine, except for the body having been touched.

Banned from the classroom, I kept one ear to what the police were telling each other, and the other to the bystanders, especially my classmates. It was 4:05 P.M., and by now, even the latecomers had arrived. Everyone was bug-eyed, talking excitedly about what had just happened, what was still happening. Except for me and Mac, I was sure that none of them had ever been at a murder scene before.

The cops seemed to be waiting for someone to arrive. I heard the name Krakowski mentioned, and grimaced, hoping it wasn't the same Lieutenant Krakowski who'd been in charge of the "Scream Museum" case— the murder Mackenzie and I had solved at the American Museum of Natural History several months back. We'd gotten on Lieutenant Krakowski's bad side back then, and she'd gotten on ours. Not our favorite law-enforcement personality.

It was she, all right. Not ten seconds later, Lieutenant

Helen Krakowski walked onto the crime scene and into the case. My heart sank. She hadn't changed a bit. Her black hair was still cut in a demure china-doll style that looked at odds with the multicolored Guatemalan jacket she wore over her regulation police duds. And her voice was even more grating than her fashion sense.

"Who's in charge of this mess?" she barked. Every cop within earshot stopped what they were doing and paid attention. "Well, listen up. From here on in, this case is mine. You can start reporting to me now."

She looked around the room, and that's when she caught sight of me. "Oh, brother," she growled. "Not you again." She stared up at the ceiling. Then she motioned me over to her with a fat, crooked index finger.

"Hi, Lieutenant Krakowski." I couldn't help staring at her not-so-faint mustache. It looked as if it had gotten bushier. "How's it goin'?"

"You wanna tell me what you're doing here?" she said, arms crossed.

"I'm in Professor Dunaway's class," I explained. "I mean, I *was*. . . ."

"Just my luck," said Lieutenant Krakowski. Her thin fish lips curled into a sneer. "Look, kid. Just because you got lucky before, doesn't mean you've got what it takes to be a detective. It takes training, discipline, smarts—"

"Looking for the murder weapon?" I interrupted. "It's outside, at the foot of the tree that faces the classroom window."

Lieutenant Krakowski gave me her dead-carp stare. "You know what? Maybe I'll have you held on suspicion for a while, just to get you out of my hair."

Luckily, she was distracted by a sergeant, who began filling her in on what the investigation had uncovered so far. "Don't go anywhere," Krakowski warned me over her shoulder.

"Hey, Riordan!" she shouted at a big, bearded officer. "Round up everyone who was in the building, or outside it, at the time of the incident, and put them in that empty classroom over there till we get to them."

Riordan got right to it. Soon, Mackenzie and I, along with Bernie, found ourselves in extremely close quarters, with fifteen of our classmates, plus custodians, other students, professors, and a few unfortunate passersby. Altogether, maybe fifty of us were crammed like salted anchovies into a room built for twenty, with the radiators banging and filling the room with hot air.

Mac was standing next to Bernie, who was seated at a desk in the corner of the room, staring into space like a zombie. Mac shot me a look that told me she was worried about her. When I motioned for Mackenzie to come nearer to the door, where I was wedged into a corner, she whispered something in Bernie's ear before doing so.

"She's catatonic," Mac whispered in my ear.

"The last thing she needs is to be grilled by Lieutenant Krakowski," I said.

"Krakowski! Oh, no, don't tell me!"

"Yes. It's true."

"She'd better go easy on Bernie," Mac said, "or I'll . . ."

"You'll what?"

Mac sighed, tossing her hair over her shoulder. "Pluck her mustache. By the way, I showed the crossbow to a sergeant."

"The footprints too?

"That's a positive."

"Good. Now, if they'd just get on with it. . . ."

Krakowski, bless her heart, kept us steaming in there for over an hour before she started calling people in for questioning. By that time, a shrink from the psychology department had arrived and started doing grief counseling. Mac and I left Bernie in her care when Krakowski called us in for our grilling.

We braced ourselves. The lieutenant was not only a real chick with a stick and as mean as a wombat, but she wasn't even very good at her job. In the "Scream Museum" case, Mackenzie and I could never get her to consider our idea—later proved correct—of how the crime had been committed. She had her own theories, and up to now, she had a perfect record: they were always wrong.

For some strange reason, Krakowski had chosen to conduct her interrogations in the classroom where the murder had taken place. Thankfully, though, in the back of the room, because Professor Dunaway's corpse was still lying there in front of the blackboard, only half hidden by a sheet.

For Mac and me, however, Krakowski's macabre decision was an unexpected bonus, a second look at the crime scene when our heads were clearer. We entered via the classroom's front door so we could see the body up close. But it was hard to get a really good scope at the corpse, which was now surrounded by police photographers, fingerprint dusters, and evidence gatherers.

As we walked by, the knot of people hiding Dunaway parted for a second, long enough for me to see something I hadn't noticed before: chalk marks on her sleeve. Our late professor was holding a piece of chalk tightly clutched in her dead hand, as if she'd been writing on the board just before the arrow had hit. I nudged Mackenzie. "Look!"

There was an equation written on the board, just next to the spot where Professor Dunaway had been impaled. It was simple algebra: $x = \sqrt{9} \times .0257906$. And it definitely didn't look like Dunaway's fluid handwriting up there on the board. "Someone *else* wrote that for her to solve," I whispered to Mackenzie. She whipped out her notebook and started copying it down.

"Hurry it up," snapped the lieutenant. As we walked down the aisle toward Krakowski, I spun through the entire scene in my mind as it must have happened: Professor Dunaway comes into the empty room. The window is wide open, but that's nothing unusual.

The radiators always made the classrooms unbearably hot. She sees an equation written on the board and starts to erase it, but for some reason, doesn't. Instead, she picks up a piece of chalk and starts to solve it, placing herself right in the line of fire. She hears a noise outside, turns, and . . .

The whole thing shook me up. Despite Professor Dunaway's cruel nature and her power tripping, she had still been a human being. Someone with feelings, hopes, and dreams. No one deserved to die the way she had died. *No one.*

"All right, you two," Lieutenant Krakowski brayed, interrupting my thoughts. "Let's hear it. And this had better be good."

5

Sinister Intentions

I'll tell you why I think Krakowski really can't stand the fact that Mackenzie and I get involved in murder cases, or any cases for that matter. She knows Mac and I will use deception, guile, ruses—anything and everything to find the killer or crook. No Miranda rights for us. Of course, sometimes we risk being arrested for invading homes, offices, or cars—sort of trespassing or a little breaking and entering—but nobody's perfect.

"Do you really think we're suspects?" Mackenzie asked, leaning back in her chair and eyeing Krakowski warily. "Even after we helped you out that time at the museum? Get real, my mom is the city coroner."

"Yeah, you're suspects, just like everybody else," Krakowski shot back. Then she softened slightly. "Look, I'm not denying you guys helped out in the wacko case at the museum."

"For which you got all the credit, thanks to us not saying anything," I blurted out.

Krakowski scowled. "Hey, I saved your lives. You should be grateful." A smile crept over her face. "But

I'm not mad or anything. I got my promotion, and the bigger bucks that goes along with it. I'm willing to let bygones be bygones and start fresh here."

It was all Mackenzie and I could do to keep our mouths shut. I think I would have said something unwise if Mac hadn't been crushing my big toe with the heel of her shoe.

"So for now, I'm going to give you the benefit of the doubt. But I want to know everything you know, and I mean everything, understand? No holding out. Where you were at the time of the murder, what you were doing, and every little thing you've noticed since then."

"Okay," I said. "We were in the computer lab with Bernadette Lello, who's in our class, doing homework, when we heard what must have been the shot."

"And did you notice what time it was?" Krakowski asked.

"Of course we did," Mackenzie said, insulted. "It was three-forty-six on the computer-lab wall clock, and my watch said the same thing."

"Very good," Krakowski said. She jotted down the time. "I expected no less from you. Go on."

"We ran into the classroom, and people were already standing there, screaming. Professor Dunaway was impaled to the blackboard, the arrow right through her chest," I continued.

"Who was there that you knew?" Krakowski probed.

"Only us and Bernadette," Mackenzie said. "It was early

for class, so none of the other kids had arrived yet. Just people who happened to be going down the hallway."

"So you three have got an alibi," Krakowski noted. "We're examining the weapon and the footprints, you'll be glad to know. Now, tell me what you think happened."

I laid out my theory of the assassin in the tree. "If the murderer jumped to the ground after firing and abandoned the weapon, he or she could have gotten away easily."

"Mmm, not much help there," Krakowski said, frowning again. "So who do you think did it? Who had a motive that you know of?"

"Well, there's a girl in our class, Gabby Zoole," I said. "I don't know that she had any more of a motive than the rest of us—"

"The whole class kind of hated Professor Dunaway," Mac explained.

"But Gabby has this hobby . . . she's into medieval weaponry. That's what we hear, anyway."

"Interesting. Anyone else?" Krakowski asked. "Any kids who hated her particularly?"

"Jeremiah Jones was having a real feud with her," Mackenzie said. "She was threatening to flunk him so he couldn't get into Harvard."

"He actually threatened her a couple times," I added.

"Really!" Krakowski jotted some notes on her pad. "Jeremiah Jones, eh? Anyone else?"

"Um, we overheard a couple of arguments between Dunaway and parents," I said. "Gabby's father, Harry Zoole—they were fighting over some investments the school made with his company."

"Mm-hmm . . . ?"

"And Burton Lello. His daughter Bernadette is the one who was with us at the time of the murder. She's only eleven," Mac said.

"Eleven?"

"She's kind of a genius," I explained. "Anyway, her dad was mad at Dunaway because she didn't treat her like anything special, the way he thought she should."

"I see," Krakowski said. "That's it?"

"I think so," I said.

"We'll let you know if anyone else comes to mind," Mac promised.

Krakowski said, "Four suspects if I count parents and kids."

"Oh, you might check out Natalie Baker too," Mackenzie said. "She's Jeremiah's girlfriend, and they're pretty tight."

"Okay, I will. Meantime, you two had better hang around, at least till I interview the suspects and see about their alibis."

"Could we stay in here with you?" Mackenzie asked. "You know, listen to you question witnesses? We might notice something."

"Something I don't?" Krakowski asked. "Not likely.

How long have you two been playing detective? I've been at this business for sixteen years."

"No offense," I countered, "but we know these kids. We might be able to tell if they're lying or telling the truth."

Krakowski scowled. It was a good point, and she knew it. "All right," she said gruffly, "but just keep quiet and take notes. I don't want you messing things up for me."

First, Krakowski interviewed Dean Beidenbach of the math department. We learned that Professor Dunaway was a workaholic who seemed to have no private life. Of course, Mac and I knew different, having overheard Dunaway's conversation in the park with Harry Zoole. We hadn't mentioned that part to Krakowski, though. With someone like the lieutenant, it's best to save some stuff for the right time—sort of like bait, so that she'd let us stay involved in the case.

Anyway, according to the Dean, the only people who ever hated Dunaway were her students and their parents. I saw no reason to argue with that.

Lieutenant Krakowski kept probing. Surely, there was a jilted boyfriend? Faculty enemies? Someone wanting to kill her who had nothing to do with the university? Dean Beidenbach kept shaking his head no. Finally, Krakowski gave up that line of questioning and turned her attention back to the list of suspects.

It was 5:30 P.M. by the time the questioning really got

started. By this time, Professor Dunaway had been carried away in a body bag, but the blood was still on the floor. Not a lot, but enough to make nearly everyone do a double take as they came in to be questioned.

Gabby Zoole was the first kid on Krakowski's list. She got a grilling about her medieval weapons collection, but held up pretty well, and denied any involvement in the crime. According to Gabby, she'd just bought a hot dog from a vendor on Amsterdam Avenue when the big clock in the chapel struck the three-quarter hour chime at 3:45 P.M. Lieutenant Krakowski told her they would check out her alibi, and sent Gabby home.

In contrast to Gabby, who'd maintained her composure throughout her interview, Bernie Lello was still so freaked out that she was barely coherent. Krakowski could see there wasn't much point in questioning her. After getting confirmation that Bernie had been with Mac and me at the time of the murder, Krakowski mercifully let the poor kid go back to the grief counselor across the hall, until her father arrived to take her home.

At around 6:00 P.M., Burton Lello stormed in. Clearly, he didn't take kindly to his daughter being questioned. "Look, my little girl is a wreck!" he yelled, his face growing as red as his carrot-colored hair. "She's emotionally fragile, and you had no right to question her without me here. I'm calling my lawyer!"

"Go right ahead," Krakowski said. "Just tell me where you were at three forty-six this afternoon."

"What for? You don't think I had anything to do with this!"

"Just answer the question," Krakowski snapped.

"Very well. I was eating a late lunch at the Plaza Hotel's Oyster Bar."

"With . . . ?"

"Alone," he replied. "But I'm sure someone will remember my being there."

"We'll see," Krakowski said. "And you ate what?"

Lello thought for a second. "A dozen Gulf oysters and the blackened swordfish."

"What was the special for the day?" she asked, her penetrating eyes on him.

"It was . . . mahimahi, I believe," he said. "Yes, I'm quite sure of it."

"All right, Mr. Lello," the lieutenant said. "You can take your daughter home now. We'll be in touch."

As soon as Lello was gone, I took the opportunity to bring something else to Krakowski's attention. "Lieutenant," I said, "about that equation on the blackboard—"

"What about it?" she asked. "Look, I've got more important things—"

"I think it may be important," I said.

"And why is that?"

"I can't say, really. I just think—well, it wasn't Dunaway who put it on the board. It's not her writing."

"So?" Krakowski gave me an impatient look.

"Well, I think she was solving it. She had a piece of chalk in her hand, and she was standing there alone by the blackboard, so—"

"So what?" she said. "She's a math teacher, right? I mean, *was* a math teacher. What else would she be doing?"

I knew this made sense, but it still bothered me. "I was just thinking maybe it was put there on purpose. You know . . ."

"Well, it sure didn't get there by accident." Krakowski rolled her eyes. "Look, just because a math equation was put on the blackboard of a math classroom proves nothing. Nothing at all."

"Well," I told Lieutenant Krakowski, "I personally think it's a lot fishier than Burton Lello's oysters."

Double-Cross Examination

Krakowski looked like she was ready to smack me, but she turned to the sergeant. "How many more on the list?" she asked.

"That we've got here? Two, Lieutenant," he said. "Jeremiah Jones and Natalie Baker."

"The boyfriend and girlfriend—okay, send her in first."

The sergeant went to fetch Natalie. She came in with her usual oh-so-superior attitude. "Okay, what?" she said, plopping herself down at a desk.

Krakowski scowled at her. "Where were you at three forty-six this afternoon?"

"At the Lion's Den," Natalie said, naming a popular pub and café on campus that was frequented by Columbia students and teachers. "With my boyfriend."

"That would be Jeremiah Jones?"

"Uh-huh."

"Hmmm . . . a very convenient alibi for the two of you, isn't it?"

Natalie shifted uncomfortably, and started to drum on

the desktop with her fingertips. "We were there. Ask anybody who works there."

"What did you order?"

"We both had burgers, and then I had an ice-cream soda."

"And you were there the whole time?" Krakowski pressed on.

"Yes, we were." She stopped drumming and her fingers clenched so hard that her knuckles had turned white. "Can I go now?"

"For the moment," Krakowski said, dismissing her.

"She's lying," Mackenzie said after Natalie had left the room. "Did you catch her body language?" Mac is an expert in this field, having learned a lot from her dad, the famous shrink. I'm not really up on the specifics, but in this case, I had to agree. Natalie had acted nervous. *Guilty.* Even Krakowski had noticed.

"She's hiding something, all right," the lieutenant said. "Don't worry, we'll worm it out of her. Or him."

In walked Jeremiah Jones. "Hey! You've got no right to hold us here. My parents have a lot of contacts in this city, and they—"

"I've got every right," Krakowski said. "Shut up and sit down, and tell me where you were at three forty-six this afternoon."

Jeremiah sat. "We were in the Lion's Den. We only found out about the murder when we showed up here for class at four o'clock."

"What did you order at the Lion's Den?" Krakowski asked him, rapid-fire.

"A . . . a burger."

"And your girlfriend, what did she have?"

"Um . . . a burger, too."

"What else?"

"What else? Um . . ."

"After the burger. For dessert!"

"Dessert . . . ?"

"Yes!"

"Um . . . she had . . . cheesecake, I think . . . yeah, that was it. Cheesecake."

There was a stony silence. "Or maybe it was ice cream. I . . . I can't remember exactly."

"Oh? Why can't you remember? Weren't you there when she ordered?" Krakowski jumped all over him.

"I was! It's just, you're making me so nervous."

"What do you have to be nervous about? You were there the whole time, weren't you? Weren't you?"

"Yes! Yes! I'm telling you!" Jeremiah was shaking now, not at all his usual smug self.

"Take him outside and bring *her* back in," Krakowski ordered the sergeant. "And make sure they don't talk to each other."

Natalie was brought back for an encore. "You might as well tell us the truth right off the bat," Krakowski told her. "We've got your boyfriend cold."

Natalie wobbled unsteadily, and sank into a chair. "Wh-what do you mean?" she asked.

"He left the restaurant early. We already know that. Now you're going to tell us what time he left the Lion's Den, and where he went."

"I—I don't know what you're talking about!" Natalie said in a breathy voice, sounding like she'd had the wind knocked out of her.

"Yes, you do—and don't lie to me again. I've already got you down for one count of false testimony. Are you going to let him drag you down with him?"

"He didn't kill her!" Natalie protested weakly. "I swear he didn't!"

"How do you know? You weren't there, were you?" Krakowski zeroed in. "You were still at the Lion's Den when he came back to kill Professor Dunaway!"

"He didn't, I tell you!" she shrieked. "He couldn't have! He wouldn't have!"

"So he did leave the café before you!" Krakowski said, leaning over Natalie.

"I want to speak with my lawyer," Natalie said, and then crossed her arms, indicating she wasn't going to say anything else.

"I can have you put away for withholding evidence, missy. Prison's not a fun place for a pretty girl like you."

Natalie's eyes welled up with tears, but she didn't say anything. Krakowski looked up at the sergeant. "Get her out of here and bring him back in."

Jeremiah passed Natalie at the classroom door, saw the mascara running down her cheeks, and charged toward us. "All right, leave her alone! She didn't do anything. I'm the one who asked her to lie."

"Would you like to tell us about it?" Krakowski offered.

Jeremiah sat down, and ran his fingers through his spiky hair. "I left the Lion's Den at three-fifteen to go talk to Dunaway," he explained. "I wanted her to let me do makeup work to boost my grade back up, so I could get into Harvard on my own merit, without my parents doing her favors."

"Favors?" Krakowski's eyebrows rose. "What kind of favors?"

"You know, like inviting her out to our house in the Hamptons for the weekend, flying her to a conference in the Bahamas, stuff like that. My parents are on the board of trustees with Professor Dunaway."

"Really?" Krakowski was making furious notes now.

"Yeah, but that didn't seem to cut any ice with Dunaway. She was a spiteful witch, but I didn't kill her. You've got to believe me!"

"Tell us what happened when you went to see her this afternoon," Krakowski said.

"She was in her office, getting ready for class," Jeremiah said. "I asked her about makeup work, like I said, and she laughed in my face. She said I was like all kid losers—'Gimme, gimme, gimme'—and that what I really wanted was to get a gift pass into Harvard. I tried to convince her I was serious about working up my grade, but she wouldn't let me."

"And that's when you killed her?" Krakowski asked.

"No way!" Jeremiah shot back. "I was done, man. I just turned around and walked right out of there. I got back to the Lion's Den around three-forty, and hung out there with Natalie until it was time for class. And when we got here, there she was—dead. I mean, I'm not sorry she's dead, but I didn't kill her."

"Did you get that all down?" Krakowski asked the sergeant. Getting a nod in return, she said, "Take him downtown for more questioning."

"What about the girl?" the sergeant asked.

"She can wait," Krakowski told him. "Let her sweat it out, and we'll see if she's got anything else to tell us, like what this one told her when he got back to the café."

"I didn't kill Professor Dunaway!" Jeremiah repeated, his voice rising now. "You've got to believe me!"

"Get him down to the squad car," Krakowski ordered. "I'll meet you downstairs in five." Still protesting, Jeremiah was escorted out of the room.

The holding room was almost empty now. Police officers were taking statements from the last few students and other witnesses. Krakowski headed down the hallway, with the two of us just a step behind. "I'm just going to check in on how they're doing in Dunaway's office," she told us. "Then I'm out of here. We've got our murderer."

"Wait a minute!" Mackenzie said, mirroring my own disbelief. "You're not going to charge Jeremiah with murder, are you? On what evidence?"

"He lied about his alibi, and got his girlfriend to lie, too. He was the last known person to see Dunaway alive, and he admits to arguing with her. Motive and opportunity, both plain as day."

"And what about the weapon?" I asked. "Are you telling me he had the argument with Dunaway, went and got a crossbow, climbed the tree, and waited for Dunaway to go into the classroom and stand by the blackboard? And that after shooting her, he left the weapon and footprints behind, and went back to finish his hamburger?"

"Exactly," Krakowski said, the irony of my words going right over her head. Giving me her tight little sea-bass smile, she entered Dunaway's office. Inside, the place was still swarming with detectives. "Find anything special?" she asked them.

"Not yet," the detective in charge told her.

"Lieutenant," Mackenzie said, "would you mind if P.C. and I hung around for a while, and maybe had a look around the office when your people are done?"

Krakowski looked like she was going to give us a fast "No," then wavered. "Why not? Cooper," she said to the detective in charge, "these two kids are amateur crime fighters, and they lucked out once—maybe they'll luck out again. Give them access to the office files, whatever else is here."

"Whatever you say, Lieutenant," Detective Cooper said, giving us a wary once-over. "You're the boss."

Krakowski smiled. "You got that right, fella." She scratched her mustache, turned, and left the room. Mackenzie and I went over to the only window, and looked down onto the quad. Krakowski stepped out of the building and climbed into the waiting squad car, sitting in the backseat next to Jeremiah. We watched as it pulled away, lights flashing, past startled onlookers and through the venerable iron gates, taking Jeremiah to the lockup.

"She's a little quick on the trigger, don't you think?" Mackenzie asked me.

"That's putting it mildly," I agreed. "She really jumped the gun."

"I don't know, though. Jeremiah *could* have done it. He's mean, and sneaky, and underhanded, and he had to admit he left the Lion's Den and went to see Dunaway."

"That doesn't mean he killed her," I pointed out. "Yes, Jeremiah's all the things you say, and he did lie about his alibi, but I can understand why he would do that, can't you? I mean, it doesn't look too good for him, does it?"

"Sure doesn't."

"Personally, I don't think he could have done it," I said, sitting on the windowsill. "He wasn't smart enough, you know what I mean? Whoever did it planned it all down to the last detail."

"I see your point," Mackenzie had to admit. "Of course, Gabby Zoole could have done it."

"In a New York minute," I agreed. "And she's the one most likely to have a medieval crossbow lying around the house, wouldn't you say?"

Searching

The police were finishing up their search of the office. "If you want to have a look around, this would be the time," Detective Cooper told us. "We're gonna be taking a coffee break for a few minutes." Cooper was tall and skinny, maybe about fifty. He had intense little blue marbles for eyes, and looked like the kind of guy who'd sit around for months wondering why labels tell you that top-loading washing machines require more detergent than front-loading ones.

"Have you found anything so far?" I asked him.

"Nothing much," he said with a shrug. "Just this letter."

He passed it to me, and Mac took a look over my shoulder. *Dear Professor,* it began.

In spite of the fact that my daughter has been acknowledged and certified as a prodigy by MENSA and other prestigious organizations, you have publicly disparaged her genius status. This could have a disastrous effect on her future. Bernadette has many

admirers who have followed her interviews on TV,
radio, and in the press. Bernadette uses the publicity
she gets to help promote worthy environmental
causes, as you know, and these, too, will suffer if she
is prevented by you from attending Columbia this
fall. Therefore, I must ask you to cease and desist
from harrassing, bullying, and emotionally battering
her in class. I do not use these words lightly, for this
is exactly what you have done. I expect an explana-
tion from you at the Faculty Tea this Sunday.
Otherwise, I shall have to take more drastic action.

Yours truly,
Burton Lello.

It was certainly as damning a piece of evidence as anything Krakowski had against Jeremiah. I wondered if it
would make her think twice about arresting him.
Probably not. Once Krakowski had zeroed in on a
subject, it was almost impossible to get her to admit
that she could be wrong. When she bit into something,
it was like a bulldog. This, Mac and I knew from
experience.

The police finally went on their break, and the two of
us got right to work, searching files and desk drawers,
and looking anywhere else we could think of. Mac and
I had one advantage over them—we knew the people
involved, and that gave us a slightly better idea of what

to look for. We divvied up stacks of files to look through, and started working, while outside the door, Detective Cooper munched on a doughnut and slurped coffee.

"Hey, here's something interesting," Mac said after a couple minutes. "It's Bernie's IQ test results. She's a genius, all right. Her IQ is one eighty-five!"

"Wow," I said. "Still, it's just a number."

"No, but there are notes here in the margins. Look."

The notes were in Dunaway's fluid handwriting, and they made clear her suspicion that Bernadette Lello was more fake smoke than real magic. "Has many limitations in native math skills," said one notation. "More skillful in taking standardized tests than in anything else."

"I think we ought to show this to Detective Cooper," Mackenzie said. "It matches right up with that letter from Bernie's father."

"You think it could be him?" I asked.

"Possibly," Mac said. "Remember how rabid he was at that Faculty Tea? He's got a real temper."

"Mmm. But this wasn't exactly a crime of passion," I pointed out. "Not the work of a hothead who couldn't control himself, but of somebody who was simmering deeply, quietly, at Professor Dunaway for a very long time."

Mac grunted in agreement, and we kept poring over files. Finally, one caught my eye. It was labeled "Americom Fidelity," the name of Gabby Zoole's father's investment firm. "Hey, Mac, check this out," I said, spreading the contents of the folder out on the desk.

There was a glossy brochure, and several pages of statements. I picked up the brochure first. It was a prospectus, listing all the benefits of investing with Americom Fidelity, and the kinds of things they did with your money. Harry Zoole was listed as Chief Investment Advisor as well as Chairman of the Board. I noticed Dunaway's familiar scribbling in the margins: "Conflict of interest?"

The address of the company was One Chase Plaza, Suite 1222. "Fancy downtown digs," I muttered, showing it to Mackenzie along with Dunaway's notation.

"Check these statements out," she said, holding up the pages she'd been reading. The first month's statement showed an initial investment by Columbia University of three million dollars, which now, three months later, had grown to 3.3 million. A ten-percent gain in only three months. I figured the projected annual growth at forty percent, compounded: a fantastic return.

But Dunaway didn't seem to think so. In her scrawled margin notes, she wrote things like: "Where are the figures?" and "Doesn't tally with Dow and Nasdaq averages for October."

Mac gave me a meaningful look. "What does this say to you?" she asked.

"It looks to me like Dunaway was gathering evidence to pull the plug on Americom. Remember the argument we overheard between her and Zoole?"

"She said she was expecting a detailed statement," Mackenzie recalled. "P.C., these are not exactly what you'd call detailed. They're more like advertisements for what a great company Americom is. No wonder she was ticked off at Zoole."

"She threatened him about some committee, too. It sounded like she was going to talk to them about pulling the university's funds out of Americom, remember, Mac?"

"So Zoole killed her to keep her from going to the committee?" Mackenzie considered this, playing with a strand of her blond hair. "It's definitely a motive, on top of whatever was going on between them romantically. And if Gabby kept crossbows around the house, it would have been easy enough for him to grab one."

While Mac was talking, I flipped through Professor Dunaway's notebook. Her lesson plans were meticulous and detailed. Not at all like Americom's "statements."

I saw where Dunaway had written down her intention to use the example of the flight of an arrow. How ironic.

"Hey . . . what's this?" Mackenzie had been flipping through the brochure, and a piece of paper fluttered to the floor. I picked it up and read it out loud:

"'Dear Mr. Zoole: I must ask you to restrain your daughter Gabby. Her behavior over the past week has been unacceptable. Even actionable. In fact, I intend to ask for a restraining order against her if she does not stop stalking me. I don't think I need to list the several instances I've spotted her hanging around outside my apartment building. You and I have already talked about this. This is your last warning. I do not intend to walk around fearing for my safety. Your daughter needs professional help. Please see that she gets it immediately, or I will bring charges against her and against you as an unfit parent. Sincerely, Eva Marie Dunaway.'"

"Whoa," Mackenzie said. "Now that's a new angle. She's a real romantic!"

"The police missed it."

She held the brochure up. "I missed it myself the first time I paged through it."

"Mac, what about him? Harry Zoole was romantically involved with Dunaway, but she broke it off with him, then she threatened to withdraw Columbia's money from his firm, and now this stuff about Gabby. Do you think—?"

"I overheard Krakowski before, yakking with one of the sergeants. She said they talked with Zoole over the phone, and that he claims to have been on the subway, alone, on his way to meet with a client."

"That's pretty thin."

"It's as good as Gabby's," Mac pointed out.

"So," I said, drumming my fingers on the desk. "Gabby Zoole . . ."

"I think we ought to have a look at her weapons collection," Mackenzie said. "What about you?"

"Good idea," I agreed. "But it's almost seven o'clock. It might be kind of late to head up to the Bronx. I mean, we've got school tomorrow morning. Besides, your folks will be wondering where you are."

"True. And I don't know about you, but I'm starving."

"Cosmic Café?" I said.

"Nah, too far away," Mac said. "I'm hungry right now. Let's go to the Lion's Den. It's right here, and we can ask about Jeremiah's and Natalie's alibis."

"Great. It'll be Gabby's right after school tomorrow."

After handing over what we'd found to a grateful Detective Cooper, Mac and I headed straight for the Lion's Den. A really sweet redheaded waitress named Irene told us she'd seen Jeremiah and Natalie hanging there that afternoon. Unfortunately, Irene was not that sure about the time. She couldn't remember when the two of them had come and gone, but she did say Jeremiah had gone out, and then come back a while later, looking flushed and upset.

Fifteen minutes later, Mac was chowing down on a veggie burger, while I attacked my usual hamburger with the works. As we ate, we added up what we'd found out so far.

"Jeremiah does look kind of caught in the act," Mackenzie commented. "But the crossbow points to Gabby, and her alibi isn't exactly airtight, either. I mean, there must be a dozen hot-dog vendors in the area, and I'll bet none of them would remember Gabby. She doesn't exactly stand out in a crowd, except for her NRA buttons."

"Look, Mac, this was a carefully planned execution," I said, going over my notes. "Whoever shot that crossbow had done their research. They knew the classroom window would be open, or else they went in there beforehand and opened the window so the arrow could be fired through it. They also had to know Dunaway would be there at three forty-six P.M."

"And it had to be someone strong enough to climb twenty feet up a tree, and get down again and away, without being seen," Mac added.

"Right. They would have waited in the tree for Dunaway to come into range, made sure no one could see them, and fired. And the tree was an evergreen. So even though most trees on the quad wouldn't have hidden the killer, this one did."

Mackenzie nodded. "Careful planning, like you said."

I tapped on the table with my pen. "Still, you'd think someone would have seen the shooter jumping down from the tree. At that hour, the quad is full of people coming and going."

"The killer probably waited till the coast was clear, then walked off casually so as not to attract notice."

"And left the crossbow at the foot of the tree. I guess

that makes sense. Walking down the quad with it would definitely have gotten some attention."

Mackenzie took a bite of her veggie burger and thought this over. "So?"

"I took the liberty of writing down the addresses of all our current suspects," I told her, flipping the pages of my little notepad. "The Zooles are in the Bronx. . . ."

"Riverdale," Mackenzie said. "Myrna said Gabby told her they live in a big house near the Hudson River."

Now, if there is one thing I know about homes, it's this: home is where people's lives are dominated by lust, power, greed, and lies. I couldn't wait to get a look at the Zooles' place.

"Riverdale's a pretty fancy neighborhood," I said. "Makes sense, especially since her dad's company is doing so well. The Lellos live on West End Avenue, Jeremiah's on Central Park West, and Natalie's on West Eightieth."

"Hey, good work!" Mackenzie said. "Plus we should check out Mr. Lello's alibi at the Plaza Hotel's Oyster Bar. We could do it on our way back from the Bronx."

"Okay."

That settled, we both went back to scarfing down our dinners. But something was still bothering me. "I know the stuff about stalking Dunaway makes it look bad for Gabby, on top of the fact that the weapon was a cross-bow. But why would Gabby use a crossbow to kill

Dunaway, and then leave it to be found on the ground? If it was such a carefully planned murder, wouldn't Gabby realize that would point suspicion directly at her? She couldn't be that dumb, could she? I mean, everyone in our class is pretty smart. Even Jeremiah."

"So . . . ?"

"So maybe some dude's trying to frame her," I said. "It could even be one of those weirdos in our calc class, like the one who makes crazy eyes out of the o's in 'school' or the girl who makes meowing sounds without moving her lips. You and I are the only sane ones."

"Yeah, right," Mackenzie said, humoring me.

8

One and One Make Three

I barely paid attention at school the next day. I was going over and over the events of the day before. I just couldn't get the image of Professor Dunaway, pinned to that blackboard, out of my mind. Lunch? Didn't eat much. No appetite. Besides, the cafeteria's special looked like roadkill à la mode.

Mac and I rode the subway uptown after school, looking at the dramatic view of upper Manhattan and the lower Bronx. The sun was setting over the Hudson River and the George Washington Bridge, washing everything with an orangy glow. It was beautiful. Too bad Mac and I were on our way to investigate a murder suspect. You gotta love New York.

We got off at the first stop in the Bronx. Gabby lived on West 232nd Street. "Number five forty-two," I said, reading from my notepad. We headed west, up the hill that led to Riverdale, a neighborhood with lots of trees, and Tudor-style houses with yards mixed in with doorman apartment buildings. Pretty quickly, I noticed that something was wrong.

"Hey," I told Mac, "we're in the six hundreds, and the numbers are going up, not down."

"Gabby must live on the other side of the tracks."

"That's not Riverdale at all," I said.

"Come on. Maybe it is, technically. We'll see."

As the street lights blinked on, we went back down the hill to Broadway and crossed under the elevated tracks. The neighborhood on this side looked like a place where Gypsy rednecks had chosen all the lawn decorations. There were mostly old buildings, the kind where the halls smell like freakazoid home cooking and there are no elevators, let alone doormen. Most of the houses were attached, and had pieces of their gutters popping off.

"This isn't Riverdale," I said. "Sorry."

"Maybe Myrna got it wrong."

"Or maybe Gabby lied about where she lived. Maybe she wanted to give the impression her folks are richer than they are."

"But her dad's got that investment company," Mackenzie said. I gave her a dubious look, and she shrugged. "So maybe it's a new company, or maybe her parents don't like to show off their wealth."

"We'll see. Here we are." I looked up at an old wood frame house, narrow in front, and long down the side. It had a front porch, and a skinny, potholed driveway leading to a garage in back. "After you," I said, gesturing. "The serial killer Son of Sam lived around here, you know. I think it was Yonkers."

"Thanks a lot," Mackenzie said, mounting the steps warily. She rang the doorbell, and medieval chimes sounded inside. After a moment, Gabby opened the door. Her face registered total shock. "What are you two doing here?"

"Well, actually, we've been asked by the police to help out on the Dunaway case," Mac said.

"Oh, yeah?" Gabby said warily.

"We're trying to learn more about the murder weapon. It was a medieval crossbow, and Myrna told us you were an expert about stuff like that," I said.

"She said you had an awesome collection," Mac added.

"Myrna," Gabby said, frowning. "Myrna's got a big mouth. She told me about *you* two being some kind of snoopy sleuths."

"Well, she's right about that," I said.

"She's right about me, too," Gabby admitted. Then her brief smile disappeared. "So you're looking into the murder, and you think I did it."

"No, we didn't say that," I protested.

"Never mind. Come on in. I've got nothing to hide." She opened the door wider and we went in. "Sorry about the house. It's a mess." I guessed she was wondering if we'd heard her brag about living in Riverdale.

"It's fine," I said, though it smelled like she was fermenting a few dozen old eggs for dinner.

"Can I offer you anything?" she asked with a phony smile. "Diet Coke or a raspberry Snapple?"

"No thanks," I said.

"So what do you want to know," she said.

"Well, to begin with," Mac said, "do you have any idea where a person could get their hands on a medieval crossbow, even an imitation one?"

"Come on," Gabby said, exasperated. "You want to know if it was mine."

"Was it?" I asked.

"No, it wasn't. I mean, I've got a few bows from that period, even a couple crossbows, but they're down in the basement."

"Could we have a look?" Mackenzie asked.

Gabby turned on her in a fury. "Why? Because you think I killed her?"

Mackenzie, as usual, had a ready comeback. "Because if you're innocent, you have nothing to be afraid of. And maybe we can help you prove it. Maybe together, we can even catch the real killer."

Mackenzie has a lot of good intuition, psychic ability, and is a great listener for gossip. And she's really terrific at adopting a loving, nurturing mode, especially if it's going to make someone say something they shouldn't.

Mac's reply caught Gabby by surprise. She stopped to consider, then relaxed, exhaling. "Oh, okay. Like I said, I've got nothing to hide. Come on."

She led us back outside, and down the driveway to the rear of the house, where there was a set of metal cellar doors set diagonally into the rear of the building. Gabby threw them open, revealing a staircase leading down into darkness. "Follow me," she said, and we did, slowly and carefully, feeling our way until Gabby found the light switch and flicked it on.

Suddenly, we found ourselves standing in the middle of a medieval torture chamber. All around us, hanging from the walls, were manacles, spikes, maces, swords, daggers, and yes, crossbows. In the center of the large room was a flat table with gears.

"What's that?" asked Mac.

"It's a rack," Gabby said matter-of-factly. "You know, for stretching people. And that's an iron maiden over there." She pointed to what looked like a round phone booth, except that the door, which was open, had long spikes on the inside.

"Egads," I said, fascinated and repelled at the same time. "Is it authentic?"

"Nah, it's just a copy. The real thing would be too expensive, you know?"

"Are they all copies?" Mackenzie asked, looking around.

"No, I've got a few genuine articles. Some of the swords and maces, a couple of longbows. Every once in a while, I find something authentic that I can afford at a swap meet or flea market. And some, like the crossbows, are copies that are pretty old themselves."

"This is quite a hobby you've got," Mackenzie said, a little too chirpily.

"Thanks," Gabby said, not sensing any irony in Mac's tone. "I even carved some of the wooden things myself." She showed us a few shields and crossbows, all authentic-looking, and very much in the same style as the murder weapon. Mac and I looked at each other, eyebrows raised. If Gabby did have something to hide, she was doing a really good job of not acting guilty.

"Hey, wait a minute. Where's—"

Whatever Gabby had been about to say was interrupted by a loud thumping from the darkness at the top of the stairs. Then a familiar voice yelled, "Freeze! Police!" and Lieutenant Krakowski came galumphing down the steps, followed by three beer-bellied officers with their guns drawn and pointed at us.

We all threw our hands up into the air. "Don't shoot!" Gabby screamed.

Krakowski stopped when she saw me and Mackenzie. "I should have known you two would be here," she said, giving us her trademark Medusa look.

"Actually, I'm surprised to see you, Lieutenant," I said. "I thought you already had your man."

Krakowski did not take kindly to my remark. "Wise guy," she muttered. "It just so happens that Jeremiah Jones has been released for now. One of the custodial workers, a lady named Alicia McGhee, claims she was sweeping out in front of the Math Building at three thirty-five when Jeremiah came out, walked across the quad, and ducked into the Lion's Den. That corroborates his story. And unless he grabbed the crossbow, doubled back, climbed the tree, and shot Dunaway, all in twelve minutes or so, I guess he's in the clear. Which brings us to you, missy," she said, turning to Gabby Zoole.

"Me?" Gabby said, her hand covering her throat.

"We have proof that it was *you*," Lieutenant Krakowski said.

"You . . . you . . . just get out!" Gabby shouted, suddenly springing to life. "All of you! Get out of my house! You have no business being here, so leave!"

"I'm afraid we do have business here," Krakowski countered, fishing a piece of paper out of her pocket and holding it up. "This is a search warrant." She turned to the other officers. "Two of you, go on upstairs and look around." The pair bringing up the rear went puffing back up the cellar stairs.

Krakowski surveyed the walls hung with weaponry. "Quite a collection you've got here." She walked over to a blank spot on the far wall. "Looks like something's missing." She traced the dust line that edged the bare spot. "Something shaped like a crossbow."

"Someone must have broken into the house," Gabby said quickly. "I just came down here for the first time in two weeks, and noticed there were pieces missing from my collection."

"A crossbow?"

"Two or three of them," Gabby admitted. "A quiver of steel bolts, too."

"I see. You say somebody must have broken in. I'm surprised you don't put in at least a cheap security system, with so many valuables to protect."

"I was going to, actually," Gabby said, looking at the ground now.

"Baloney," Krakowski said.

"It's possible she's telling the truth, Lieutenant," I said.

"Stay out of this, kid," Krakowski said. "When I want your opinion, I'll give it to you. And that goes double for you," she warned Mackenzie, who already had her mouth open to defend me.

"You might be interested to know," Krakowski told Gabby, "that we've gotten a report from our weapons expert." Brandishing a handful of papers, she continued, "She says the murder weapon was a hand-carved copy of a medieval crossbow." Krakowski looked intrigued as she started to read from the expert's report. "'The weapon has been modified to house a high-caliber gun shaft, capable of firing the steel bolt that struck the victim, in much the same way that a modern harpoon gun might work on a whaling ship.'"

"So the modification would give the weapon increased power and accuracy?" I asked.

"Less finger pressure on the trigger," Krakowski said. Then she turned to Gabby. "Speaking of fingers, there's something else about the murder weapon. Your fingerprints are all over it."

Gabby began to choke.

"Yes, we were able to match your prints to a set we already had on file."

"My God, that was years ago. I shoplifted a few lousy videos from Blockbuster, for crying out loud! But I didn't kill Professor Dunaway. Don't you see, someone's trying to make it look like I did!"

Krakowski came right up to Gabby and stared into her pale, frightened face. "Your mother left the country two weeks ago, didn't she?"

"Yes . . . so?"

"Was it over your father's relationship with Professor Dunaway?" So Krakowski had found out about that in spite of me and Mac.

"My God, no! She's just on vacation!" Gabby said, but her tone was so shrill that it was obvious she was lying. "Who do you think you are!"

"You hated Dunaway for breaking up your parents' marriage, hated her so much that you stalked her for a week. And then you murdered her!"

"No!" Gabby broke into tears as Krakowski towered over her. The two policemen came back down the stairs. One of them nodded to Krakowski, holding up his prize, a muddy pair of Timberland boots.

"Why were you outside Professor Dunaway's window?" Krakowski demanded to know.

"I wasn't, ever! Ever!"

Krakowski examined the boots. "These look like

they'll match the footprints in the mud around the tree," she said, nodding.

"I hate to butt in, Lieutenant—" Mackenzie started.

"Then don't."

"But anyone smart enough to modify that crossbow wouldn't be dumb enough to leave the evidence behind. Especially the murder weapon with her fingerprints on it, or muddy shoes that match the footprints at the murder scene."

Krakowski stared her down.

"Sorry," Mackenzie said. "I just had to say it."

The Lieutenant turned her attention back to Gabby. "Professor Dunaway notified you and your father that if you didn't quit stalking her, she'd haul you into court."

"Sure," Gabby said, her eyes blazing now, "I tried to talk to her at school, but she always raised her voice and embarrassed me in front of everyone. I thought if I could catch her walking her dog or something, maybe she'd listen to me. I just wanted her to leave my dad alone, stop persecuting him."

Tears choked off her voice, but Krakowski remained a perfect refrigerator. "You had the motive, you had the means, and you had the opportunity. None of the hot-dog vendors we've interviewed remembers you, so you have no alibi. Your fingerprints are on the murder weapon. And these boots look like they'll match the footprints at the base of the tree. I think we've got plenty to go on, here. Boys, take her downtown."

"You're not taking me anywhere. At least not until my father gets home!" Gabby stepped back, closer to the row of swords that hung on the wall behind her.

For the first time, I wondered if she actually knew how to use any of the weapons she collected.

Krakowski didn't seem concerned. "All right. If you want me to cuff you, I will."

"Hey!" Mac protested. "She's just a kid!"

"Sure," Krakowski said. "And we've got enough kid killers nowadays to fill Yankee Stadium. Sweet sixteen, collects medieval weapons, and is old enough to be cuffed. In fact, it's the only way this kid's going to sit behind me in a squad car. I'm not crazy."

"But don't you see?" I yelled. "This is a case of *too much* incriminating evidence!"

"God, there's no pleasing you two, is there?" Krakowski snapped.

Mac chimed in. "Someone's obviously trying to frame her!"

But it was no use. We watched helplessly as the police surrounded Gabby, cuffed her, and led her out of the basement screaming.

"What do we do now?" Mackenzie asked as the flashing lights faded into the distance.

I stared around at the dark, empty street, its shadows long and menacing. "We get out of here, that's what we do."

9

Homicide on the Half-Shell

Mackenzie and I power-walked back to the subway and headed downtown. We were tired and hungry, but we couldn't get past what had just happened. "You don't think Gabby's the killer, do you?" Mac asked me as we sat on the train, headed back toward Manhattan.

"Not for a minute," I said. "She may be the kind of kid who makes her own flogging equipment with candlesticks and pinecones . . . maybe she's even a little obsessive. But she's not idiot enough to leave a trail of clues leading straight to her."

"Of course not," Mac agreed. "It's such an obvious setup. Somebody just walked into that cellar and took the stuff. They even thought to take Gabby's boots, too, and wore them to commit the murder, just so there'd be an obvious set of footprints leading back to Gabby. And they returned the boots to her closet, too."

"Hard to believe Krakowski went for it," I said.

"P.C., come on. Krakowski?"

"You're right," I said. "It's not hard to believe at all."

"So what's next on our list?" she asked.

I checked my notepad. "Got to check out Mr. Lello's alibi."

"Do you really think someone at the Plaza will remember him being there?"

"With that red hair of his? Very possibly."

We got off the subway at 59th Street and walked east to the Plaza Hotel, making our way through the luxurious lobby, around the side of the famous Palm Court, to the Oyster Bar. The hostess, a tall, gorgeous blonde in a really hot, yet totally elegant black dress, asked us if we wanted a table. By the way she was looking us up and down, I could tell she was hoping we'd say no.

"We're not here to eat, actually," I said. "We were just wondering if you remembered someone being here yesterday afternoon."

"Oh. Well, I was on duty, but we have a lot of customers. . . . Do you have a photograph of this person?"

"No," Mac said, "but you couldn't have missed him. He's really tall and thin, with red hair that's kind of wild looking, like that comedian you always see on TV who uses props like rubber chickens and whoopee cushions."

"Oh, yes, I seem to remember a gentleman like that. About fortyish?"

"Right!" I said. "Around what time was he here?"

"He must have come in around two-thirty or so, I think."

"And how long did he stay?" Mac asked.

"Well, I would think an hour or more, but I couldn't tell you for certain."

"That would have made it impossible for him to get uptown in time," Mac said. Turning to the hostess, she asked, "What was the special yesterday?"

"Let's see. It was mahimahi, braised with teriyaki sauce."

That matched what Lello had said the day before. "Do you happen to remember what he ordered?" I asked the hostess.

"Yes," she replied. "He made an awful fuss."

My eyebrows rose, and so did Mac's. "What kind of a fuss?" I asked.

"He claimed the oysters he ordered were bad, upchucked one into a napkin, and started shouting about it. Those oysters weren't bad at all—he'd already eaten five of the dozen, and then he had the nerve to demand that we bring him a dozen clams instead. We get customers like that a couple of times a month. You know, they're basically stealing food, and I resent it."

"Yeah, the nerve of some people," I said sympathetically. Did I mention she was totally hot?

Mackenzie yanked my sleeve. "Come on, P.C. Let's get moving."

We thanked the hostess and left the Oyster Bar, heading back out into the street. It had started to rain, so we stood under the hotel's awning, waiting in line for the doorman to flag us a cab to take us home. "No doubt about it," I told Mac. "Lello was here. His alibi holds up."

"What bothers me," Mackenzie said, "is that it sounds like he made that fuss just to establish an alibi for himself."

I shrugged. "Possibly. But there's still no way he could have got up to Columbia in time to shoot the arrow out of that tree."

"You're right," said Mac.

We didn't talk any more about it, but Mac's words continued to crawl around in my mind. I just couldn't figure out why.

While we were waiting, Mac's cell phone rang. "Hi, Bernie!" I heard her say. "How are you doing? Feeling any better?" She held the phone up close to my ear so I could hear Bernie's reply.

"I'm okay now," she said. "In fact, I got to thinking maybe I could help you guys find out who did it. You know, be detective partners like we talked about."

Mackenzie and I exchanged a dubious glance. The last thing we needed was a needy eleven-year-old tagging along with us everywhere we went. On the other hand, Bernie had an excellent brain. She was definitely a whole lot smarter than either of us had been at that age.

Bernie didn't wait for an answer, but went on. "You know Gabby's dad? He has this investment company or something? Well, at the faculty tea, he gave my dad some brochures, trying to get him to invest with him?

So I saw in there that Mr. Zoole went to Georgetown University? I called their alumni department, and they never even heard of him!"

"Bernie, are you sure?" Mac said, as surprised as I was.

"Oh, yeah, I'm sure," Bernie said. "So I was thinking, if he lied about where he went to college, what else is he lying about? Probably a whole mess of things."

"Right," I agreed. "But what made you suspicious of him in the first place?"

"Well, I noticed that every time I've seen him, he strokes his nose."

Mac blinked. "So?"

"Have you ever heard of the Pinocchio syndrome?"

"No," I said. "What is it?"

"'The stress of lying causes tissues in the nasal passages to fill with blood. The noses of liars become sensitive and they repeatedly touch or even pull at them.'"

"Omigod," Mac said. "You've carried the analysis of body language to a whole new level!"

"Not me," Bernie said. "The FBI. They did that study in nineteen thirty-six."

Bernie had sounded like she was reading out loud. I wondered if she was, or if it was that photographic memory of hers.

Now she continued in her normal voice. "Mr. Zoole is a liar, guys. He might even be the killer!"

Mackenzie and I stared at each other.

"So what do you think?" Bernie asked, breathless. "Can we be partners?"

Mac looked at me, and I shrugged. "Sure, Bernie," Mac told her. "Keep up the good work. We'll check out Mr. Zoole right away."

"Cool! What should I do next?"

"I'm sure you'll figure out something," I said. "Thanks, Bernie. We'll touch base soon."

"Wow," Mac said after we hung up. "How long do you think it would have taken us to call Georgetown and check out Harry Zoole's credentials?"

I shrugged. "Bernie's smart, all right. Dunaway was wrong about her."

"So what do you think? About Harry Zoole, I mean?"

"Well, he's certainly a phony," I said. "What if Dunaway's theories about him and Americom are on the money?"

"Is that supposed to be a pun?"

"Sorry, couldn't resist. But really, Mac, he has just as much access to Gabby's weapons as Gabby does. Maybe he's cooked up some kind of convoluted, vicious plan. I mean, his alibi isn't much of an alibi, alone on the subway. Maybe he's desperate, and doesn't care who he incriminates."

"His own daughter?" Mackenzie asked.

"Look at it this way. Dunaway was so mad that she broke it off with him, and she was threatening to look closer into his business dealings. Maybe he decided to kill her. Maybe he stole one of his daughter's crossbows, knowing the police might think it was his daughter, but figuring eventually she'd be cleared. I mean, who knows what he's planned?"

"I agree," Mackenzie said. "There's something lost-in-the-sauce about Harry Zoole. And Krakowski's always been one to jump the gun. First Jeremiah, then Gabby. The whole time we were up at her house, Gabby didn't give one single indication that she was guilty. When Krakowski led her away, my scalp was spazzing."

The taxi line had been moving along while we were on the phone with Bernie, and now it was finally our turn. A cab pulled up to the curb, and we stepped out from under the awning. Just as we were about to dive into the backseat, the streetside door of the cab was yanked open, and two people shoved in from the other side.

"Hey!" Mac shouted. "This is our cab!"

And then we saw who had jumped the line—Jeremiah and Natalie! Their matching leather bomber jackets were wet from the rain, and they looked more startled to see us than we were to see them.

"Excuse me," the doorman said, leaning into the cab, "this line is for hotel customers only."

"Cry blood!" Natalie yelled at him. Taken aback, the doorman just stared at her.

"Never mind," I told him, "we'll share."

"Very well, sir," he said, backing off.

I closed the door, and tried to get comfortable in the crowded backseat. It was useless. "Can I ride up front?" I asked the cabbie.

"Sorry," he said in a thick Russian accent. "Not supposed to let. Four in backseat against law, too."

"So, don't look," Natalie told him.

I sighed, and scrunched up some more. Mackenzie, trapped between me and Natalie, looked even more uncomfortable. The two cab-stealers were taking up at least two-thirds of the backseat.

"Where you want go?" the cabbie asked.

"Two eleven Central Park West," Jeremiah shot at him, before either Mac or I could say a word.

"Honestly," Natalie said, batting her overly mascaraed eyelashes. "I wish you guys would stop bothering us. Just because that idiot policewoman let you stay in the room while she interviewed us doesn't mean that you're Scotland Yard or the CIA."

"We weren't following you around," Mac replied, annoyed. "*You* jumped into *our* cab, remember?"

Jeremiah ignored that piece of news. "Let me save you both a lot of time," he said, leaning across Natalie so he was right in our faces. "I didn't do away with Dunaway, because I didn't have to. I tried to get her to recommend me to Harvard, and she wouldn't, but my dad has a lot of friends in high places. There are ways of getting into the Ivies that have nothing to do with SAT scores and demented professors like Dunaway."

"Yeah," Natalie piped up. "People like her don't know what real power is in this world."

"It's called money," Jeremiah said. "My dad was always ready to buy me a place in Harvard's freshman class. I wouldn't have had to kill anyone. So keep your mouths shut about what happened yesterday. The last thing I need is for it to get around that I was a suspect in a murder case. Nothing's going to stop me and Natalie from being together. Got it?"

Happy that he had put us in our places, he turned to the cabbie. "That building on the corner," he said, pointing out a fancy prewar building with two uniformed doormen out front. "It's been nice talking to you both," he said, giving us a nasty smile. "Come on, Natalie."

"You know, Jeremiah," I said, "you two deserve each other.

"Yeah," Mac seconded. "A hubba dweeb and his jockin' dingbat."

They grunted, got out, and it was only after they were gone that I realize they'd stiffed us for the fare.

Sum People

The next day was Friday, and since our last period was study hall, Mac and I were able to get permission to leave school early. We wanted to check further into Harry Zoole's activities. A phone call was all it took to find out that the head of Columbia University's Institutional Investing Committee was a Dr. Ernest Kaufman. We phoned ahead and made an appointment to see him at 3 P.M.

Entering Euclid, we passed by our empty calculus classroom, which was still cordoned off and guarded by a policeman sitting at the door. There were two other forensic technicians inside, gathering fibers, dust, and hairs—the infinitesimal bits of evidence that can't be seen with the naked eye, but that make it possible to get more and more convictions these days. DNA doesn't lie.

Dr. Kaufman, an older man with a curly fringe of white hair circling his large head like a halo, was waiting for us in the faculty lounge. He got straight to the point. "What exactly are you looking for?" he asked.

"We're interested in knowing more about Americom Fidelity," I said.

"And Harry Zoole in particular," Mac added.

"Well, I can assure you that Mr. Zoole is a very trustworthy, competent investment counselor. Columbia wouldn't have turned over a seven-figure check to him if he wasn't."

"You gave him three million of the university's funds to invest?" Mac said.

"Yes," Kaufman confirmed. "It was Professor Dunaway who first brought him to the committee's attention. Then she suddenly seemed to grow suspicious of him." He sighed. "Look. Eva Marie was always devoted to, and perhaps overprotective of the university's funds and its reputation. When it came to anything to do with math, and especially financial matters, she was a genius."

Egads. There sure were a lot of geniuses connected to this case! "Well, sir, I don't mean to sound disrespectful," I said, "but if Professor Dunaway was a whiz in that area, weren't you concerned that she was suspicious of Mr. Zoole?"

Kaufman shrugged. "To be candid, and I don't mean to speak ill of the dead," he said, "Eva Marie had, shall we say, a rather difficult personality. She was quite abrasive, and there were many people she didn't get along with. Mr. Zoole, I'm afraid, came to be one of them."

"You mean there were lots of people who disliked

her," Mac said. "And one, at least, who disliked her enough to want her dead."

"Apparently so."

We got nothing more out of Dr. Kaufman. Mac said she thought he was from a time warp, and I had to agree. I would have bet that he and Dunaway hated each other's guts. Their personalities would have been like oil and water, and he wouldn't have liked her challenging his financial judgment. Zoole had obviously charmed him, and I had an idea why. Americom had returned over ten percent on Columbia's investments in just three months, while in that same time, the stock market had dipped more than five percent. Zoole was doing well by Columbia. So why did Dunaway remain suspicious of him? And why did Mac and I agree with her?

Back out on the quad, I pulled out my cell phone, flipped open the mouthpiece, and checked in with Jesus Lopez, our good buddy and top computer brain. "Hey, Jesus! How goes it?" I said.

"P.C.! *Cómo va, amigo?*" his high-pitched voice came back.

"Pretty good, pretty good. Mac says hi, too."

"Cool. Back at her."

"Listen, we're working on a case, and we need your help."

"Excellent! What can I do for you?"

I filled him in on the murder, and asked him to check for anything unusual he could find out about Harry Zoole and Americom Fidelity. "And by the way," I added, "see if you can find out where his wife went for her vacation. All I know is that she flew, and she headed south."

"You got it, man. I can hack into the airlines' computer records, no problem."

"And while you're at it, Jesus . . ."

"Yeah?"

"Could you check and see if you turn up anything freakazoid on a Burton or Bernadette Lello?"

"Sure thing. I got it covered. Back to you later."

"You're the best, Jesus," I said.

"You know it," he agreed.

After I pocketed my cell phone, I saw that Mackenzie was looking at me funny. "What?" I asked.

"Why do you want him to check on Bernie? She was with us when Dunaway was killed. She's got a great alibi. Us."

"I know," I replied. "Just habit, I guess. I don't want to pass over anything."

"Oh." Mac backed down. "But in that case, we shouldn't count creepy Jeremiah out as a suspect either, in spite of his supposedly airtight alibi."

"I couldn't agree more. I wouldn't trust that snob as far as I could throw him anyway. He could fake out anyone, including that custodian who gave him his alibi."

"I don't like him and Natalie wearing matching out-fits, that's what I can't stand," she said. "So tacky. It makes me nauseous."

We were on the subway now, headed back downtown. It was noisy, and since that kind of put a damper on conversation, I fished out my little notebook and looked over everything I'd jotted down so far about the case. When I got to the equation I'd copied from Mac's notebook, I stopped. It had been tugging at me since I first saw it. It wasn't just the fact that someone had used it as bait so Dunaway would be in the right place for a clear shot. There was something else about it, if only I could figure out what.

"Hey, Mac," I said. "Got your calculator with you?" She fished in her backpack, and pulled out her trusty old "Sharpie."

I studied the equation: $x = \sqrt{9} \times .0257906$. In other words, $3 \times .0257906$.

Mackenzie punched the numbers in on her calculator. With a shrug, Mac showed me the result: $x = .0773718$. "It doesn't mean anything, does it?"

"It certainly didn't mean much to Krakowski, either."

She cracked a smile. "I don't think police like to do math."

I studied the equation again, this time with the answer written in. "It does seem straightforward. But something tells me it isn't. Remember, it was in a weird hand-writing we didn't recognize, Mac, as if someone had written it with their left so no one would be able to identify it as their work."

"Why would anyone bother?"

"To lure Dunaway to the spot so they could zap her."

"But what is there about this equation that would intrigue her so much she'd just have to solve it?"

I thought I knew who might be able to figure it out. "Let's stop at Bernie Lello's and see what she thinks of it."

I found her address in my notebook. It was on West End Avenue in the Eighties. We got off at 86th Street and Amsterdam and walked west. It was four o'clock, and already, the sun was setting over the New Jersey Palisades. That cold wind whipped in from the Hudson River again, making us shiver.

Bernadette and her father lived in a classic West End Avenue high-rise, the kind of building where all the apartments have parquet floors and high ceilings, and the walls are made from real plaster, not the cheap, thin drywall they use in newer, more crumby buildings. The concierge called upstairs for us.

In the elevator, I got to thinking about Bernie, and what her life must be like. "It must be scary, you know, being a genius like her. I mean, to have an intellectual capacity like Mozart or Einstein, or Bobby Fischer. She probably even hears the music of the spheres."

"There are different kinds of genius," Mac said. "Maybe Dunaway was jealous of Bernadette. Maybe she was selling Bernie short because of some personality conflict or envy. Maybe Bernie was everything Dunaway herself had wanted to be. . . ."

Bernadette opened her apartment door for us. She seemed happy to see us, but I could tell she was still shaky. Who wouldn't be? And after all, she was only eleven. No matter how smart you are, seeing a dead body that close up, with an arrow sticking right through it, could not be easy to shake off. There was a lot of sauce on that pizza, let me tell you. I had seen dead bodies before, and even I was still flashing back to the sight of Dunaway pinned to that blackboard.

"My dad went out to dinner with Jay Leno's people," Bernie said. "I'm supposed to be on his show Christmas week."

"Jay Leno?" Mackenzie said. "Can Oprah be far off?"

"That's okay," I said. "It's you we wanted to see anyway."

Bernie looked ecstatic that we'd called for her. "I was just updating my Web page," she said, boastfully. "Jazzing it up, you know. Wanna see?"

"Sure!" Mac said, with an encouraging smile.

Bernie led us to her computer desk. On the screen, her home page, ablaze with new, colorful graphics, blared out at us:

BERNIE'S GIRL GENIUS HOME PAGE
GREETINGS, PILGRIM,
YOUR SEARCH HAS ENDED!

The menu options offered included:

BERNIE'S SOCIETY TO SAVE THE TIGERS OF BANGLADESH
BERNIE'S CRUSADE TO HELP FEED THE HUNGRY
 CHILDREN OF AFRICA
SCHEDULE OF UPCOMING APPEARANCES
BERNIE'S PHOTO GALLERY

Mackenzie clicked on the photo gallery. "Awesome," she said.

Bernie's face lit up like a magnesium flare. I thought Mac was overdoing it a bit—overcompensating for how creepy we thought the site really was. There were photos of Bernie in all sorts of active poses: riding an elephant; marching in a Greenpeace parade; standing next to cardboard cutouts of her dad and a woman who must have been her mother.

I studied this last picture, and Bernie saw me looking at it. "I don't see my mom much anymore," she said. "But dad puts her mock-up in there for promotional photos, just to give everyone the idea we're still one big happy family. He'd be in the shot for real, except then it would look weird that my mom wasn't."

"Where is your mother, Bernie?" I asked, thinking even as I spoke that I should probably have kept my mouth shut.

Sure enough, Bernie's eyes started welling with tears. "She's . . . gone away," she whispered, choking up. "Daddy says she's never coming back."

"Poor baby," Mackenzie said, patting Bernie's shoulder. "How have you been holding up? No nightmares or anything?"

Bernie shrugged, and shook her head. "Not really. Not that I can remember. But I have had trouble getting to sleep."

I could believe it. She had dark circles under her eyes, and she kept yawning. I thought I'd better show her the equation before she fell asleep.

After looking at it for less than ten seconds, she said, "It's just a straight equation, as far as I can see. Why?"

"It was on the blackboard when Dunaway was shot," I explained. "She was trying to solve it."

"Oh." Bernadette didn't seem to get the significance of this. "Have you checked into Mr. Zoole yet?" she asked instead. "Because my instincts are you should do it sooner rather than later." She nodded firmly, as if to emphasize the point.

"We're sort of in the middle of doing that," I said. "We're waiting on a phone call, actually. We just thought we'd stop up here on our way and see if you could help us with the equation."

Bernie looked at the equation again. "The answer is .0773718. So?"

Mac and I looked at each other in amazement. She didn't even need a calculator. "Does it mean anything to you?" I asked.

"Nope. Sorry," she said. "Listen, I could go with you

wherever you're going to check out Mr. Zoole, but my dad would probably have a coronary if I wasn't here when he came back. I wish I was a few years older." Resting her chin in her hands, she stared back at the photo of her with her "mom and dad" on the screen.

I figured it was time to leave her alone, so I told her we had to be going. "We'll call you if we find out anything about Zoole," I promised as she showed us to the door.

"Okay. Thanks!" She waved when we stepped into the elevator.

As we descended, Mac said, "She's taking things awfully well, considering."

"I guess she is," I said. "She may be repressing her emotions, though. She seemed kind of weirded out."

"She seems confident that Zoole did it, doesn't she?"

"Yeah, I did." I chewed on my lip for a moment as something else hit me. "You know what else I noticed?"

"What?"

"She wasn't wearing her special glasses. You know, the ones to cut down the glare from the computer screen."

"So?" Mac shrugged. "Maybe she got tired of using them, or they didn't work so well after all. Or maybe she lost them or sat on them?"

"I guess." The elevator doors opened at the lobby and we got out. "Still, you'd think after her dad spent so much on a pair of special glasses, she'd take better care of them."

"She's had a lot on her mind," Mackenzie reminded me.

"True, true. More than any eleven-year-old should have to go through," I said. "This whole case is beginning to give me an advanced case of the creeps."

Wrong Division

It was already 5:30 when we got to the One Chase Plaza building, a long ride downtown by packed rush-hour subway, but a cab at that hour would have been big bucks and impossible to get. Probably, like most people, Zoole had closed up shop for the weekend at five.

Mac and I went into the lobby. We found the electronic directory, and punched in Americom Fidelity to get the dial-up code. No listing.

Mac and I looked at each other. "Looks like Bernie may have been right about Zoole," I said.

"Okay," I said, "Let's try looking under suite twelve twenty-two, the address on the brochure." We did, but the system wouldn't let us look it up that way, so we went over to the information desk.

"Americom Fidelity?" the lady behind the desk repeated, acting like she'd never heard of it. She checked her computer, shook her head, and told us what we already knew. "Doesn't seem to be any listing."

"It's supposed to be in suite twelve twenty-two," I said.

A knowing look came over her pudgy, tired face. "Ohhh," she said. "Suite twelve twenty-two. Why didn't you say so in the first place? Sign in here."

"You mean we can just go on up?" Mac asked, surprised.

"No problem."

"And they're open?" I asked.

"They stay open till nine P.M., Monday through Saturday."

"Hmmm," I said as we got in the elevator. "Strange business hours for an investment company."

Even stranger was the sign on the frosted-glass door of suite 1222: ZIPPY FREIGHT AND MAILING SERVICE, INC. It opened onto a tiny, hole-in-the-wall office, with a long tablelike separation between customers and the firm's employees. Said employees at this hour numbered exactly one: a small, bald man with Coke-bottle glasses. He was squinting over some papers, and didn't look up when we came in.

"What kind of place is this, anyway?" Mac asked.

"I think," I replied, "and I stress that it's only a guess—I think this is the kind of place where a person, or a firm, can rent a mailbox, so it *looks* like they have an office."

"What?" Mac said, scowling. "You think Americom Fidelity is just a front, P.C.?"

"I think we should check and make sure," I said. "Distract that guy, so I can look it up on his computer?"

The man looked up at us, and cleared his throat. "Yes, can I help you?"

Mac turned to him and gave him a big, toothy smile. "You sure can!" she said, meeting him at the barrier. "Do you rent mailboxes?"

The man smoothed down his nonexistent hair. "What size were you looking for?"

"Why don't you tell me what you have available," Mackenzie said.

Seeing that the man was safely distracted, I ducked under the barrier and snuck over to the desk where his computer sat. I fiddled around till I got SEARCH, then typed in "Americom Fidelity." The screen changed to read: "BOX #43032, $20 per month, paid through December. Forward all mail to Harry Zoole." Zoole's home address was listed, along with his phone number.

I'd seen all I needed to see, and signaled to Mac. I knew she wouldn't appreciate it if I made her keep up her scam any longer. She didn't mind using her looks as a weapon, so long as it was aimed at someone she thought was hot. This guy definitely didn't qualify.

"Well, I'll have to think it over," she said, backing away from him just as I popped back up on the customer side of the barrier. "Bye, now." She waved, then scooted out the office door.

The man waved back, smiling dumbly. Only when the door closed behind Mac did he notice me. "Er, yes sir?" he asked. "Can I help you?"

"I'm with her," I explained, getting to the door as quickly as possible. Poor guy. Now his fantasy was totally ruined.

"Well?" Mac asked as we raced down the hall to the elevators.

"Zoole's company is nothing more than a mailbox! I'll bet the only reason for Zippy Freight and Mailing's existence is to make phony companies look like real businesses."

"I can't believe people fall for that."

"Not just people—*smart* people," I pointed out. "Like Dr. Kaufman."

Mac said, "But not Professor Dunaway or Bernie Lello."

"Well," I said. "I guess we'd better alert Krakowski."

"And Kaufman, too," Mackenzie said. "He'd better hope Columbia's money isn't already gone!"

Back out on the street, we tried to flag down a cab. The trouble was, all of them seemed to be taken. Finally, Mac stepped out into the street to try and wave one down. Just then, my cell phone started playing 'Smells Like Teen Spirit.' I pushed the talk button. "Hello?"

"It's Jesus, guy."

"Hey! How's it going?" I said. "Mac and I just checked out Americom Fidelity. The address is phony! It's just a mailbox service."

"I found out that the company isn't even registered,"

Jesus said. "And Harry boy has been sending funds to a bank account in Buenos Aires."

"Argentina?"

"No, the Ukraine. Yes, of course, Argentina! What do you think?"

"Egads," I said. "Sounds like major scamming."

"And he's got an account here, too," Jesus added. "At the Chase branch on West Seventy-third Street and Broadway. It's got a balance of several hundred thousand dollars. Sounds to me like the dude has been keeping Columbia happy for the past few months by paying out made-up dividends from the money they gave him. Meanwhile, he's squirreling most of it out of the country."

"Which means," I interrupted, "that Zoole himself will probably be cutting out mucho soon."

"Wait, I'm getting to that," Jesus said impatiently. "You asked me to check out where his wife went for vacation? Same place, dude."

"Buenos Aires?"

"Uh-huh. She left a few days ago, right before the professor lady got kabobed."

"Jesus, listen to me," I said, as Mac came over to see what was up. "I want you to check and see if Zoole's bought any airline tickets yet."

Jesus shot back, "I already checked. He and someone named Gabriella Zoole have seats on American Airlines flight four-oh-three, out of JFK, at eight-thirty tonight."

"Tonight!?"

"Are you having a hearing problem or something? Yeah, tonight at eight-thirty. JFK."

"Jesus, do you think you could have called a little earlier? It's already six-thirty!"

"No lie? P.C., time flies when you're having fun."

I hung up, just as Mac succeeded in flagging down a cab by practically hurling herself in front of it. We jumped in, and I shouted, "JFK Airport! And I'll double the fare if you get us there in a hurry, but without any major collisions or killing anyone."

The cabbie, a wizened man in a white turban, stared at me in the rearview mirror. "What I can do?" he said. "Street is full of much traffic. Never mind. I get there fast."

"Great." I turned to Mackenzie and opened my mouth to say something. Just then, the cab screeched into motion, lurching to the left across three lanes of horn-blaring traffic, hung a U-ie to head back downtown, and made straight for the Brooklyn–Battery Tunnel entrance.

"Whoa!" Mac said. "No tip if you kill us!"

"Not to worry," the cabbie replied with a brilliant white smile. "I get there fast!"

12

Blood Money

Our driver, Mr. Patel, was one of the last true Punjabi cowboys. I never knew it was quicker to go through the back streets all the way across New York than to take the highways during a Friday evening rush hour. No double-parked cars, no jaywalking pedestrians, no unloading trucks could stop our careening progress toward the airport. And a good thing, too. Time waits for no man, and neither do international flights.

I knew that all airlines tell their passengers to arrive a few hours early for international flights, to give them time to negotiate customs and the beefed-up security checks. That meant Gabby and her father were probably already at Kennedy. I could only hope we wouldn't be too late to stop them from vamoosing the country.

"So," Mac said. "I guess that solves the puzzle. Zoole killed Dunaway because she was going to blow the whistle on him about his phony investments and his embezzling."

"It sure does look that way, doesn't it?" What I didn't say was that I wasn't quite buying the whole thing. Sure,

Zoole was a fraud, but that didn't necessarily mean he'd killed Dunaway. Certain things bothered me about identifying him as the killer, but it was hard to think with Mr. Patel zigging and zagging his way around screaming pedestrians and road-raging motorists. "Ha-ha!" he cried. "I'll make it in twenty-five minutes! A record! Yes! Yes, indeed!"

"You'll get the bonus if we're *alive*!" Mac reminded him.

"Not to worry, miss. I am very safe driver," Mr. Patel assured us as he slammed on the brakes to avoid smacking into an ambulance that was stopped directly in front of us. "Sorry." He giggled sheepishly, then floored it again. The ambulance attendants yelled something nasty, but we were too far away to make out what it was.

"We'd better call Krakowski," I said, pulling out my cell phone.

"What's the use, P.C.? She won't listen to a thing we say anyway."

"Maybe not, but I don't think you and I ought to try to take on the Zooles by ourselves."

"There's airport security," she pointed out.

"Yeah, but they won't know what's going on. They're more likely to believe Mr. Zoole than a pair of hyperventilating teenagers."

"I beg your pardon," Mackenzie said. "I resent that remark."

I punched in the number of the 20th Precinct and

asked for Lieutenant Krakowski, only to be told she was out on an investigation. "Well, when will she be back?" I asked.

"Couldn't say. You know how these things are. Can I take a message?"

"Yeah, you can take a message. Tell her Harry Zoole and his daughter are about to flee the U.S.! Tell her to get herself and some reinforcements out to the American Airlines Terminal at JFK, ASAP—the flight leaves for Buenos Aires at eight-forty! Oh, and see if she can hold the flight up till she gets there!"

"I'll give her the message," said the policeman on the other end of the line, sounding distinctly dubious. "But I don't know. What did you say your name was?"

"P.C. Hawke. She knows all about it. Page her now! This is totally urgent!"

"I'll do my best, but I can't promise anything."

"Fine. Thanks." I hung up, and sighed with frustration. "Why is it always like this when Krakowski's involved? I mean, she's frustrating even when she's not there!"

We were somewhere in the heart of Queens, and time was flying by. "It's seven-thirty!" Mac said, looking at her watch. "Please, can't we go any faster?"

"You want faster?" asked Mr. Patel, turning to us with a gleam of insanity in his eyes.

"Just a little," Mac said, backing down.

"Watch the road!" I screamed.

By the time we arrived at the airport, it was after 8:00 P.M. Mr. Zoole and Gabby would surely have cleared security, and were probably already at the gate, about to board their flight. Mac and I gave Mr. Patel a ten-dollar bonus, but we didn't stick around long enough to see if it was enough to make him happy. We burst into the terminal, looking every which way for a sign of our quarry.

The American Airlines hub at Kennedy Airport is a sprawling, two-building affair, which also happens to be under serious construction, part of the whole airport's "Renovation for the 21st Century." We soon found out that Mr. Patel had dropped us off in front of the wrong building, the one dedicated to domestic flights. We ran full-speed down the length of the building, dodging travelers and their bags as best we could.

"Do you think the police will be on the alert for them?" Mackenzie asked, between huffs and puffs.

"Let's hope so," I said. "And let's hope Krakowski checks her messages frequently."

When we finally got to the international part of the terminal, we looked up at the monitors for flight 403. It was listed as on time, departing from gate 35. We ran down the hall that led to the gate, only to be stopped at the security area by a uniformed guard who blocked our way. "May I see your tickets, please? Passengers only beyond this point."

I was about to argue with him, to try and explain,

when I spotted Mr. Zoole and Gabby, just on the other side of the security check. He was retrieving an aluminum briefcase when he looked up and saw us. He seemed to have trouble recognizing us, but he clearly realized we looked familiar.

Gabby had no such hesitation. She gasped loudly, grabbed her dad by the wrist, and started dragging him off in the direction of the gate.

"That briefcase!" I said, knowing immediately what must be inside it.

"Please, sir, you've got to let us by!" Mac begged the security guard.

"Sorry," he said, "Rules are rules. No exceptions."

Seizing my chance, I ducked to the left, and ran through the open area that was restricted to arriving passengers coming through in the opposite direction. "Hey!" yelled another guard. "Stop! Freeze!"

I did no such thing. And as the first guard turned to see what was going on, Mac ducked through the X-ray machine. She ran toward me, followed by half a dozen more guards, who were blowing their whistles and drawing their guns!

At this point, I couldn't see the Zooles. Had they gone straight to the gate? I tried that first, and sure enough, they were on the short line to get on board. As soon as they saw me, they took off again, heading away from the gate and up an escalator that led to a level of duty-free shops and restaurants.

I followed as quickly as I could, taking the steps two at a time. Near the top, I yelled over my shoulder to Mac, "Go down to the other end of the hall and head them off!"

"*Now* you tell me!" she yelled back, then turned and, with great difficulty, ran back down the up escalator.

I was sorry for making a fool out of her, but it was a stroke of genius, as it turned out. My escalator was at one end of a long hallway, and I figured there'd be another at the other end. If there was, Mac could get there first, and we'd have them trapped between us.

Sure enough, just after the Zooles disappeared down the escalator at the far end of the row of shops, I reached the top, and saw that they were doing a Mackenzie—trying to run back up the down escalator. They spotted me and froze, realizing the trap was sprung. In that moment, Mac caught up to them, and yanked the briefcase out of Mr. Zoole's hands.

That got their attention. Forgetting about me completely, Harry Zoole took off back down the escalator in pursuit of Mackenzie and his briefcase. Mac ran around to the up escalator, and as she passed, tossed it over to me, which caught both Zooles completely off guard.

Now they had to run back *down* the *up* escalator, and by the time they got to the bottom, I was off and running, back down the long hallway with the gates heading off either side. The security detail had stationed themselves as a cordon across the walkway to stop anyone from leaving. Seeing them, I stopped suddenly. Harry Zoole barreled into me. The briefcase went flying into the air, hit the overhanging monitor that showed departure times, and burst open.

Now it was raining money. Hundreds of bills fluttered through the air, causing everyone in sight to come running to grab their share. I searched for the Zooles in the cloud of money and the crush of people, but I'd lost them.

Finally, I managed to disentangle myself from the tangle of grasping arms. On the outside of the greedy mob, I looked toward the security gate. There were Harry and Gabby, hands in the air, surrounded by at least a dozen cops, all with their guns drawn. Behind me, security staff were busy pulling the treasure seekers off each other, and recovering what they could of the Zooles' loot.

Mac skipped up to me, grinning, and slapped me on the back. "Way to go, P.C.," she said.

A young lieutenant emerged from the crowd of cops. He put his gun away and smiled. "Lieutenant Krakowski asked me to thank you two," he said. "She's waiting for you downtown. She says you guys rule."

"What?" I said. I had heard him perfectly well, I just wanted to hear it again.

Trap!

Krakowski, for once, seemed pleased with us, not to mention with herself. It gave me a queasy feeling. Mackenzie and I had been flying on adrenaline since getting Jesus's phone call about the Zooles. Our freakazoid cab ride, our psychotic chase through the terminal. All of it had been so exciting that the ride back to Manhattan felt like sailing on a Frisbee. And now, that heady feeling was gone in an instant.

"You did good," Krakowski told us, coming out from behind her desk to give us a handshake. "We were closing in on Zoole anyway," she added, making sure the old reputation stayed shiny. "He had every reason to kill Dunaway. She was about to expose him."

My heart stumbled another inch lower inside my chest. Krakowski was jumping to conclusions again, her usual modus operandi. The day of the murder, it had been Jeremiah Jones who'd killed Dunaway. Just last night, she'd been totally convinced it was Gabby. And now Harry Zoole.

I glanced over at Mackenzie, and she put her palm on

top of her head, letting me know the skin up there was doing something. I decided to speak up before this went any further.

"Zoole *could* be the killer," I interrupted, "but don't you think he's smart enough not to use one of his own daughter's weapons of choice? I mean, obviously, he was taking her with him to South America. And from the look on her face when she saw us at the airport, I'd say she was definitely aware that her father was swindling the university. So why would he want to make her look guilty of murder?"

Krakowski stood there, staring dumbly at me. Her expression hardened. I saw her shoulders tense as she formed both her hands into fists. "Are you kidding?" she said. "That's just why he wanted to get her out of the country so fast!"

So much of what she said made no sense that I didn't know where to begin. In that moment of hesitation, Krakowski quickly strode to the office door. "Gotta go," she said. "Press conference at City Hall." She couldn't help but bubble at the thought of all the great publicity she was about to get. And she wasn't going to let any of our lame, pubescent doubts rain on her parade.

"Wait a second!" I said. "Why would he bother to kill Dunaway if he was leaving the country with all that money anyway?"

"Listen," Krakowski replied, "people get stabbed around this city for three bucks, never mind three million! So he was leaving, but it was Dunaway who'd put an end to his scam and forced him to flee the country. He was mad at her, so he killed her. End of story."

"But why would he take that risk?" I countered.

"Ha! Most criminals never think they'll get caught," Krakowski explained. She put on her cap, checked out her Guatemalan threads in the full-length mirror, then opened the door to go. "They're dreamers, most of them. They see the world through rose-colored glasses, know what I mean?"

Then she was gone, and Mackenzie and I were left to ponder her words. "Well, that's that, I guess," Mackenzie said glumly.

When I didn't answer, she looked up at me. "What, P.C.? What are you thinking?"

"I'm thinking that poor Harry didn't kill Dunaway," I said.

"What?"

"What Krakowski said about rose-colored glasses. Maybe that's how everyone's been seeing this case all along. Us included."

"What are you saying?"

"All this time, we've assumed that Dunaway was shot by someone sitting in that tree outside the classroom window."

"Yeah . . . ?"

"Well, what if *nobody* was in that tree? What if the crossbow was wedged up there beforehand, aimed at

113

the blackboard, and the recoil of the shot knocked it to the ground?"

"You mean, the killer fired it by *remote*?"

"Maybe. A tiny transmitter, in a pen. In anything."

"But they wouldn't know when to fire it," Mac pointed out. "How could they tell that Dunaway was in the right position?"

"Oh, someone knew," I assured her, the light dawning in the back of my brain. "I think I know how. And I think I know *who*."

I pulled my notepad out of my pocket. I needed to check that equation one more time. There had to be a clue there, something we'd missed the first couple times around. A tease of a solution deliberately buried by a very clever, very confident killer.

I found my scribbles where I'd written down the answer to the equation, x turning out to be .0773718. Both Mac and I stared at the numbers till our eyes began to cross.

"I still see nothing," Mac said.

"Wait a sec," I said. "Remember how Dunaway always told us we had to round off to the nearest hundred-thousandth? That would result in x equaling .07737! Do you see it?"

"Omigod," Mackenzie said. She took the pad from my hand and turned it upside down. "LELLO!" She gasped. "It spells Lello. But which one?"

"*Quién sabe?*" I said. "It's got to be one of them,

though. And we're gonna find out which."

"But it can't be Bernie. She was with us when the shot was fired. She may be a genius, but she couldn't have been in two places at once. It *has* to be her father."

"Maybe, but remember, he's got a pretty good alibi, too. And what about her mother?"

"Didn't Bernie say she was dead?" Mac asked.

"She said she was gone, and wasn't coming back. Maybe her parents are just divorced or separated."

I pulled out my cell phone, the gears in my brain shifting into trapping mode. I looked up the number on my notepad, and dialed the Lellos' apartment.

Burton Lello answered. "Hello?"

"Mr. Lello? This is P.C. Hawke—you know, from Bernadette's calculus class? We met at the Faculty Tea."

"Oh." He sounded taken aback, and distinctly nervous. "Yes?"

"I wanted to speak to Bernie about something."

"She's washing up for bed," he said. "It's after ten."

"Sorry to call so late," I said. "But could you tell me something?"

"What is it?"

"Your wife—is she . . . is she deceased?"

There was a long pause, and Lello's voice was unsteady as he answered. "She's been in a . . . hospital for three years. A . . . mental hospital."

"Oh! I'm sorry. . . ."

"It's all right. My wife is—was a genius, too, you see—

just like Bernadette. But she pushed herself so hard to succeed . . . one day, she just cracked. Fell apart. It was . . . it was awful." He was silent for a long moment, then added, "So you see, that's why I was so determined that Professor Dunaway not pressure Bernadette. I want my daughter to develop to her fullest potential, but I don't want her to end up like . . ." He stopped, unable to finish.

I cleared my throat. "Are you sure your wife is still in the hospital?"

"Of course I'm sure. What kind of a thing is that to ask?"

"When was the last time you checked, sir?"

"A couple months ago. If she'd left, they would have notified me, I'm sure. What's this all about?"

"Could you leave Bernadette a message for me?" I asked.

"What is it?"

"Tell her Mackenzie and P.C. wanted to thank her. See, she helped us with a lead on the Dunaway murder."

"Oh . . . ?" There it was again. That nervousness in the voice, that fear.

"Yes. She helped point us in the right direction. Tell her we've figured out how Dunaway was *really* killed— and that we're going to get the cops to do a *really* complete search of Dunaway's classroom first thing in the morning, now that the room's been unsealed. There's something important the police haven't found yet."

I hung up before he had a chance to answer, or to put Bernie on the line. Whichever one of them was the killer would be spooked by what I'd just said, and hopefully would do something dumb.

"Come on!" I told Mackenzie. "We've got to get up to Columbia—pronto!"

14

The Killing Ground

Fog had settled on the city, and when we emerged from our cab at the Amsterdam Avenue gates, the streets were eerily empty. There are plenty of areas in New York City that are full of people at 10:30 on a Friday night, even in December. But this was not one of them. Isolated people hurried down the street, and mist-silhouetted figures lurked in shadows and door-ways.

We had left word at the station for Krakowski to meet us here, but of course, she wouldn't go anywhere until her news conference was over—and maybe not even then. So I made sure the message read URGENT. I didn't know if our killer was going to show up, but I wanted the police to be on hand, just in case.

The quad was just about deserted, and the foot-lit, pillared buildings gave me the funny feeling of emerging from a time machine into the heart of ancient Rome. A student in a long, tan camel-hair coat scurried by on his way to someplace snug and warm. In the mist, the coat could almost have passed for a toga. A rat scurried across the path in front of us, and Mackenzie and I stopped in our tracks. "Whoa!" she said. "Talk about creepy."

"I hope the building's not locked," I said. I don't know what had made me think it wouldn't be. Sure enough, although the lights were still on in the hallway, the main doors had a steel chain strung across the handles, held together with a nice-sized padlock.

"Okay, maybe there's another door or a window open somewhere," I said. We circled around the building. On the north-facing side there was a door with no chain on it. In fact, it was propped open by a concrete cinder block. I stepped up to the door, looked inside, and quickly ducked back into the shadows. The custodian was in there, sweeping the hallway.

"We could just ask him to let us in," Mac whispered. "Tell him we forgot our books upstairs."

I thought this over. "What if he says no?"

"Good point. Never ask permission when the answer might be no."

"Right."

"So?"

"So we wait for our moment—I think it's just arrived." The custodian had put down his broom and was pushing open the bathroom door. "Now's our chance, Mac! Let's go!" We quickly ducked inside, around a corner, and headed for the nearest staircase.

The stairs, unlike the downstairs hallway, were not lit.

We found ourselves in almost total darkness, the only light spilling in through the windows from the quad outside. We tiptoed up to the second floor, where the hallway was at least lit by a dim night-light at either end. A snake of fear began to crawl up from my stomach.

Mackenzie gripped my arm too tightly. I knew that she was scared, too. Anybody would have been. The place had the atmosphere of a chilly, shadowy under-privileged crypt.

The classroom had indeed been unsealed. When I'd said that to Burton Lello, I had no idea if it was true.

We entered the room and got to work. It took me and Mackenzie a while to set everything up the way we wanted it. I wasn't sure exactly where the murderer had hidden what we were looking for, and we had to search by the light of our pocket flashlights.

Just as we were putting on the finishing electronic touches, we heard the thumping sound of the stair door shutting. We flicked off our lights and ducked behind a pair of desks. The faint, angled light from the hall bounced on the ceiling. A huge shadow appeared there, carrying what appeared to be an enormous duffel bag.

I poked my head up a few inches. The duffel bag wasn't nearly as huge as its shadow, and neither was the little girl carrying it. In the ghostly light, Bernadette Lello looked like a naughty leprechaun carrying a sack full of ill-gotten treasure.

I glanced over at Mac, whose eyes were like Pringle

can tops staring at me, as if to ask whether we should pounce right away. I shook my head no, and gave her the palms-down signal that meant "wait."

Bernie made straight for the rear of the room. We held very still, hoping she wouldn't see us—yet.

She stopped at one of the two computers that occupied the back wall of the classroom. Opening her bag, she took out a screwdriver, and used it to pry off the cover of one of the monitor's small speakers. She fished around inside.

"Looking for your camera, Bernadette?" I said, standing up along with Mackenzie and playing my flashlight on her startled face. We moved quickly between Bernie and the classroom doors. I pointed the flashlight at the ceiling, where Mac and I had taped the miniature TV camera. It looked for all the world like a cyclops's eye. "We took the liberty of moving it—and removing the signal scrambler."

"What are you talking about?" Bernie asked, recovered from her initial shock and putting on her usual mask of innocence.

"I'm talking about the remote that let you know when to fire the crossbow in the tree."

Mac, who was holding the remote we'd found, now flashed it at the three monitors we'd placed side by side in front of the room. They flashed on, each showing the same thing in close-up: Bernie's ashen-gray face, her eyes filled with growing panic.

"I don't understand—"

"Yes, you do, Bernie," I said. "I mean, I've only got a general idea from my knowledge of basic sci and physics. But you. You're a genius. You knew exactly how to pull it off."

"I don't know what you're talking about," she insisted.

"Well, let me lay it out for you, then," I said helpfully. "An ordinary, noncoherent light source—say, the image of this classroom—is converted by a special lens into a polarized one, like a laser beam. This new image is transmitted electronically to a receiver, and viewed. By you. Sound familiar?"

"No."

"In other words," Mac said, "you received the image of the classroom on the computer you were watching in the lab across the hall."

"You were there!" Bernie said. "You know I was doing math problems. You could see my computer screen yourselves!"

"Ah, but we weren't wearing your special gizmo," I said. "The glasses that allowed only you to see the scrambled image."

"You're talking nonsense," Bernie insisted. "I've got very sensitive eyes! They were a prescription!"

"Bernie," I said, shaking my head, "I'm sure no eye doctor prescribed those goggles for you. You wrote that prescription for yourself—a prescription for murder." I took a step toward her. "Oh—and we took the liberty of removing *this* from your camera tonight." I opened my fist to reveal a small black box sitting in my palm. "Your scrambler."

Bernadette's eyes were wild now, scoping the room like a trapped raccoon. "You're just playing at being detectives. I thought I would help by playing along! This is the thanks I get!"

"You were playing a different game all along," Mac said.

"You came here early that day," I said, closing in. "You wrote the equation on the board, killing two birds with one stone. You got Dunaway into position, and left the calling card of a genius, proving that she was wrong about you—dead wrong."

The wild look didn't leave Bernie's eyes. "How did I fire the weapon?"

"You preset it in the tree," Mackenzie said. "Wedged it. And you fired the weapon with a remote. You probably had the transmitter in a pen. One click, and bam!"

"There was no receiver found on the weapon," Bernie said.

"Oh, yes," I said, "that was *really* smart of you. I don't know exactly how you did that—maybe a tiny detonator at the base of the bullet charge where the receiver would be vaporized when the gizmo was fired. Anyway, kiddo, we have *you* on the videotape, prying out the camera you'd mounted in that computer, and that you thought was still there. Only the killer would have known where that camera was hidden."

Bernie reached into her bag. "One thing you're wrong about," she said. "It wasn't a one-of-a-kind weapon."

She lifted a loaded crossbow out of the bag, and aimed it straight at my head.

"P.C., look out!" Mackenzie screamed, diving. She knocked me down just as the arrow shot past my eyeballs.

Bernie was already reloading. Mac and I ran for the door, and dove just as Bernie launched another arrow. It crashed into the tile wall next to us, fracturing it and sending plaster fragments flying.

"How can she load and fire that thing so fast?" Mac said.

"Training," I yelled as we ran down the hall. With Bernadette, the pint-sized hunter, in hot pursuit, I felt like that shipwrecked guy being stalked by that crazed count in that story *The Most Dangerous Game*.

14

Final Answer

We ducked into the stairwell with Bernie still stalking us. She called down the stairs, "I know you're there. Ready or not, here I come!"

The lights on the main-floor hallway were out. We ran in the nearly complete darkness toward the door we'd entered by, but there was now a thick chain across the outside of it, and the door wouldn't budge. The custodian must have finished his work and gone home.

"The basement!" I told Mackenzie. We ran back past the staircase to the far end of the hallway, where there was another set of stairs. We raced through the door just as Bernadette loosed another arrow. It sped by us in the dark, not missing by much before slamming into another wall with a sickening, shattering noise.

Mac and I ran down the stairs and into the dark basement. The only sounds I could hear was my heart pounding in my ears. The basement, lit only by a scattering of dim yellow night-lights, was a maze of twists and turns. Huge steam pipes lined the pathways, which detoured around fuel tanks and boilers. Electrical wires hung in tangles above our heads.

"This place is a mass of fire-code violations!" Mackenzie gasped as we entered the labyrinth, trying to put distance between ourselves and our pursuer.

"Man, I sure hope Krakowski got our message!" I whispered, just before we heard the door to the stairs open, signaling the arrival of little Bernie Lello and her great big crossbow.

"Can I play with you?" Bernadette called, laughing hideously. "I'm coming. . . ."

We kept bumping into things in the shadows, which unfortunately let Bernie know where we were, but we couldn't help it. The farther we went, the darker it got, and we were moving so fast that we couldn't tell what was an object and what was a shadow. We didn't want to use our flashlights. It would have been like painting bull's-eyes on our backs.

"This is a dead end!" Mac said in a hoarse, panicked whisper.

We doubled back, took another passageway, throwing down whatever we could behind us to slow Bernie's progress—maybe even bang up her shinbones in the bargain.

"P.C.!" I heard Mac gasp.

"Don't tell me. . . ."

"It's another dead end!"

"Mac, I asked you not to tell me that."

Bernie's tiny silhouette stood in front of us. I caught the flash of a steel arrow, already fitted in place.

"I'm sure even you two can figure out the solution to *this* equation," Bernie said. "Sorry to have to kill you. You were so nice to me. But that's the way it all adds up."

"Think for a minute, Bernie," I said. "You can only kill one of us. The other will have you down before you could get off a second shot."

"Excellent reasoning," she said. "So back up—both of you. All the way back, slowly, with your hands raised."

We backed up, past rows of cartons stacked six feet high on our right, and a concrete wall on our left. Just as we passed a fire extinguisher hanging on the wall, Mac said, "Dive!"

I did, dropping to the floor like a sack of potatoes. There was a flurry of motion as Mac grabbed the extinguisher and fired it blindly in Bernie's direction. Carbon dioxide clouds billowed in the room, accompanied by a loud hissing. I still heard the twang and whoosh of the crossbow being fired as Bernie went down, screaming.

I scrambled forward, fishing in my pocket for my mini flashlight. I flailed my hands around to try and clear the clouds of vapor, and saw two figures on the ground. Mac was straddled on top of a crazed Bernie, with the crossbow kicked across the room.

"Call the cops!" Mac shouted. "Call somebody! Call her *mother*!"

We heard doors slamming above us. I helped keep Bernadette down like a gremlin and joined Mac in calling for help. It wasn't a minute or two before a dozen police officers, led by Lieutenant Helen Krakowski, charged down the stairs to us. Someone threw on the lights.

"Boy, are we glad to see you!" I said, words I thought Krakowski would never hear coming out of my mouth.

"Hello?"

"Hey, *amigo*, it's me, Jesus! Listen to what I got for you on this genius kid—"

"You're too late, compadre," I said on my cell phone. "The cops are taking her away right now."

"Oh," Jesus said, sounding disappointed. "Anyway, you wanna hear what I found out?"

"Sure, why not?" I said, holding the phone up and out so Mackenzie could hear, too, squeezed in close as she was in the back of the squad car.

"So this Bernie, I check out her Web site, and she's got a lot of future bookings. Her daddy's about to make a lot of *dinero* off her, you know what I'm saying? Pretty soon she's going to be getting big fees for TV shows and commercials—much more than she's been getting up to now. This kid's going to be a cash cow."

"*Was* gonna be, Jesus," I said. "*Was* is the operative word here. This kid's going to a kiddy reformatory for a good long rest."

"Not as long as you think, man," Jesus said. "She'll be

out soon enough. They gotta let you out when you're twenty-one. By that time, she'll be bigger."

"I hope not *badder*," Mac said.

"I mean, I'd invest in her right now, man. She's goin' places, eventually," Jesus opined. "She's going to be worth six, maybe seven figures a year. Just think of the advance on her prison memoirs alone! And her CD!"

A chill came over me as I pictured Bernie Lello's eventual release from confinement. Jesus was right. She was going to be a force to contend with, one way or another.

A few days later, Mac and I once again found ourselves in our favorite spot in Central Park, near the pond. Only three weeks had passed since our last visit, but the weather had changed drastically. It had been Indian summer then. Today, it was gray, with a cold wind and snow flurries blowing horizontal, dive-bombing the water and the concrete. The pond was starting to freeze over. The old salts and their boats had gone home.

Mackenzie had been away for the weekend with her family Christmas tree shopping, an old tradition of theirs. On Monday, after school, instead of going home or heading for the Cosmic Café Annex, we just instinctively pointed our noses toward the park, and kept walking till we got to our favorite spot. We needed to talk it all over, without the danger and tension that had been hanging over us. This was the best place we knew for doing that.

"You know, P.C.," Mac said, "I really feel sorry for Bernie. She was kind of a victim, too."

"Let's not go there," I said.

"We have to. When she was a little kid, she was probably only filled with wonder, and a promise that the world was good—until her mom fell apart, and her dad started to mold her."

"Well, that's a one-sided thought," I said. "I've got the feeling good old mom helped lay down a bit of groundwork for the little monster, too."

"Really, though. By the time we met her, Bernie was nothing more than the professional genius her father had made her. I mean, there was nobody else at home inside her, and when Professor Dunaway messed with that—threatened her whole identity—Dunaway had to be killed."

"And killed brilliantly," I added. "Which goes to show you, even tiny genius brains can be used for good or nasty."

"But the point is, even geniuses have to be taught to be evil. If you ask me, I think her dad's the one who should be going to jail. I'll bet he drove her mom crazy, too."

I sighed deeply. "I'll tell you, Mac, without the equation, I would have never guessed it was Bernie, would you?"

"It's a good thing we did, before we were dead," Mac said.

"But that's the thing about evil. It could be lurking inside anyone, even you or me."

"Hey, speak for yourself."

"No, but it's true!" I insisted. "Evil can be anybody! Someone shopping next to you might be a monster inside. Or one of your neighbors. You just never know."

"You sound like a trailer for reality TV."

"No, look, Mac. Other species kill only for food and to protect their territory or their young. Humans are the only ones who plan their killing, who kill and maim and torture their own kind for fun. Think of those machines in Gabby's basement. Somebody actually designed those thingamajigs. Somebody pretty smart."

"Depends what you mean by smart, P.C. Like you said, brains can be used for good or evil."

"Hey, Mackenzie," I said, cracking a smile. "You know what the difference is between genius and stupidity?"

"What?"

"Genius has its limits."

"Huh?"

"Think about how profound that thought is, and when you do, picture Krakowski."

Mackenzie's lips curled into a smile. She slipped her arm around my waist. I knew it was one of those times she just wanted to stroll and think about things like the amazing skyline, falling leaves, and a cup of steaming hot chocolate.

CHECK

OUT

THE

NEXT

P.C. HAWKE

MYSTERY . . .

From the terrifying files of P.C. Hawke:

DEATH ON THE AMAZON • Case #6

Case #6 began something like this:

A howler monkey's scream shattered the predawn peace of the Peruvian lowlands. Moments later another scream sounded—this one from inside the dilapidated old boat named *Inca Princess* that was ferrying me and my main buddy, Mackenzie Riggs, down the Amazon.

Inside *Inca Princess*'s walk-in freezer slumped the corpulent form of one Mr. William Donnehy: a multimillionaire Texan, obnoxious blowhard, and collector of oddities and curiosities—curiosities like the very ancient, very creepy mummy Mac and I were escorting to Lima for my archaeologist dad. His naked chest gone blue-white with the cold, Donnehy looked more like a poorly butchered holiday turkey than a captain of industry. Having your heart hacked out with a machete will do that to you.

Mackenzie and I looked around at the motley collection of crew and passengers. One of them was a vicious murderer. The jungle, teeming with anacondas, caimans, and jaguars, stretched out in a green tangle in all directions. We were hundreds of miles from the nearest police station—hundreds of miles from the nearest telephone, for that matter. It would be up to Mac and me to figure out who had carved up the late Mr. Donnehy—and avoid getting ourselves carved up in the process.

Recording the truth and nothing but the truth, I am,

P.C. Hawke

a.k.a. Peter Christopher Hawke